THE
*Tender*
KILLER
S. B. HOUGH

# THE
# *Tender*
# KILLER

## S. B. HOUGH

**PERENNIAL LIBRARY**
Harper & Row, Publishers
New York, Cambridge, Philadelphia, San Francisco
London, Mexico City, São Paulo, Sydney

All characters in this book are entirely fictitious. The Author regrets that the effect of the British libel laws is to force him to use, particularly for his less pleasant characters, names which must be common to a great number of innocent people.

A hardcover edition of this book was first published in England under the title *The Bronze Perseus* by Martin Secker & Warburg, Ltd., and first published in the United States as *The Tender Killer* by Walker & Co. in 1959. It is here reprinted by arrangement with Brandt & Brandt, Inc.

First PERENNIAL LIBRARY edition published 1984.

Library of Congress Cataloging in Publication Data

Hough, S. B. (Stanley Bennett), 1917-
    The tender killer.

    Originally published as: The bronze Perseus.
    I. Title.
[PR6058.O83B7 1984]      823'.914      83-48354
ISBN 0-06-080680-X (pbk.)

84 85 86 87 88 10 9 8 7 6 5 4 3 2 1

# CHAPTER ONE

HAROLD GEORGE ALBERT CLEMENS was a careful, intelligent, studious and up-to-date young man. There were no entanglements in his life, and few distractions. When he found himself in the small industrial town of Lepley for the purpose of examining a new production process on behalf of his employers, a go-ahead plastics firm, he regarded it simply as a period of work, and not by any means as a holiday or an escapade.

He took himself seriously, which was, of course, why he had been sent to do such an important job at a comparatively early age. He did not think in terms of dance halls, wild parties, good fellowship in bars, or even of the cinema or television. Other young men might take the opportunity of being in a strange town to discover such of these things as the locality might offer. Not so Clem. He stayed in his dismal, lonely hotel room writing up his copious notes until ten o'clock at night, and then he went for a walk entirely from a sense of consideration for his health.

He crossed the dimly-lighted hall of the hotel and let himself out through the swing door hoping that he would still be able to get in again when he came back. He felt sure he would be able to do so. Even in the provinces there was always some way to get into an hotel, at least until midnight. He saw that there was a damp, chill fogginess in the streets, which obscured

5

the more distant street lights, but also there was an autumn mildness: it was not really cold. As always, there was a considerable precision in his impression of the immediate facts.

Even at home, Clem often went for a walk at ten o'clock at night. He lived alone in a flat with pictures on the walls, a radio-gram in the corner, and books on the shelves. But usually, even at home, by the time he had finished his studies, what he really wanted was a breath of air. He had little time for fiction. He was concerned with things.

In Lepley, he walked down the street. Ahead, he saw a door open and a light shine out into the fog. Four young people emerged from what was evidently a pub and stood swaying on the pavement, not drunk but laughing and talking loudly in their local accent, unsure of their next move but reluctant to break up the party just because the pub had closed. Clem crossed the street away from them. They were still talking when he passed them on the other side, the two girls together with one man behind them and the other in front of them.

Employees, he thought. Employees of the factory he had visited that day. He did not envy them their present pleasure. They did not know where they were going. Perhaps that was the connotation of being an employee. An employee had to have an employer, and a technical staff, men like Clem, to tell him what to do.

Since there were no pubs in Clem's life, and no dances, and no careless wasting of time, there were also no women. You could not have it both ways. He was convinced of that even in Lepley. He would have a wife someday, he did not doubt it. But that would be when he was Chief Chemist at a works, and in a position to own a large suburban house, a car, and a young woman who was herself from the environment into which he would move. He crossed the road away from the possibility of the immediate gregariousness of the young people precisely because he did know where he was going in a wider sense than through the misty, night-shrouded streets of Lepley.

He thought of the last book he had read, for relaxation, before he had left his home town. It had been a book on Archaeology, and it had caught his imagination. It had been based firmly on things, on actual finds and artefacts dug up at Jericho and Ur. From those things, from battered and mislaid and long-lost objects, the experts had been able to build up pictures of whole civilisations, long since vanished. Perhaps, Clem thought, if his acquaintance with Lepley were confined to a few beer mugs, a polished door knocker such as the one he saw glinting as he passed it, and a lamp-standard such as the one he was approaching, he might do the same. Life in Lepley, for everyone except the factory manager, who anyway did not live there, was in fact dictated by such objects, which Archaeologists, if they dug them up, would classify as being of poor materials and bad design.

He did not know where the street would lead him, as he walked quickly along it. But then he did not need to know. He had a grasp of the greater issues, a geographical sense of direction as it were. Sooner or later, he knew, the houses which fronted directly on the pavement would fall back. He would find himself in some suburb with tiny gardens and houses which, crowded together, were technically semi-detached. Then he would turn right. When he had had enough, he would turn right again. All roads would lead back to the centre of the town, and his hotel was near the junction of main streets that he had just left.

Another book he had read, on—what was it?—Social Biology. The behaviour of animals, including the human animal, in the group. The social behaviour of even the lower orders, so that monkeys, and even hens, were bound to a rigid etiquette within the tribe. Peck-order and territory in birds. The people of Lepley were no different. Nine tenths of their imagined superiority over animals arose simply from the fact that they did not know how animals did behave. Their society was no more complicated than that of many kinds of ants, and their manners and courtship rituals even left something to be desired compared with those of peacocks or bower birds.

He discovered that the terraced houses had ended, that the uneven flagged pavement had given way to a smooth path of tar macadam, and that he was walking by tiny, low-hedged gardens between interrupted rows of houses most of which had lights in the bedroom windows. He breathed deeply of the cool, damp air. His forecast had been accurate, as it had been bound to be. Even the temporal pattern of the Lepley people's lives was quite predictable. Although he had not been to the town before, he realised that he could have said, with complete certainty, that few of them would go to bed before ten or half past, and almost none of them would voluntarily be awake after midnight. It was time, he thought, to look for a main suburban road that would offer him the expected branching to the right. How far had he come, a half mile to a mile from the centre of the town? He turned right, but turned too soon. The road led into another and he had to turn left again. For a short time, until he got his bearings and discovered a continuous road that led through the maze, he was entangled in the suburb.

Away to his left, at some time then, he heard a woman scream. The sound seemed to come from about two streets away, but as that part of the suburb was not laid out rectilinearly, he could not be sure. He was momentarily shocked by the intensity of the sound that rose up to the night. For a moment he half expected to hear a squeal of car brakes, and perhaps a crash. When nothing of the sort happened, he thought of sudden sickness, an accident to a child, or other form of terror. When he came to the long continuous road that he had expected to find, he looked left along it before he turned right. Lepley being a small town, it had the aspect of a lane, with trees and fields on the far side of it, the street lamps far apart, and pools of darkness in between. The fog seemed thicker there, too, whiter, and clinging to the ground as it did in open country.

He was almost sure he heard movement, a gate click perhaps, and voices talking, away there to the left. Whatever had happened was being taken care of, and he found himself glad to turn right, as he had intended, and to walk away from it.

It was not that he was unfeeling, he thought in all sincerity as he increased his pace a little as he walked along the road. The intricacies of the suburb had taken him a little farther than he intended, and now he would have to hurry a little in order to follow the lane to the next road that led back into the town if he was going to reach the hotel by midnight. He might, he thought, have told someone at the hotel that he was going out and so avoid the possibility that they would close the door thinking him in his room. But it was not that it was unfeeling to walk away from someone's evident distress. On the contrary, he was perhaps too feeling, too aware of the immediate possibility of pain in every life. When disasters happened, in his experience, there was always some capable woman, a motherly character, to lend a hand. Some person whose mind rarely moved further than the next meal, who saw things immediately for what they were, but who did not generalise them or imagine that one person's pain was significant to everyone or to the nature of the whole.

He was looking at a remarkable phenomenon when the police car passed him for the first time. He had seen that though the fog was thick on the ground in the almost country district in which he was now walking, yet he had only to look up through it to see the stars. The stars, he thought, as the police car went past, moving in the same direction as himself, not towards the trouble but away from it. They had looked down for countless generations on human misery. And not only human misery. The stars had been the same when whole species had been wiped off the face of the earth. The stars were not beings, as the poets made them, but they were matter, the common stuff that composed the universe as a whole. It was the universe that was indifferent, indifferent to the life that swarmed on one tiny portion of it, indifferent to the incalculable death and anguish that took place on the earth in every single minute. Yet he, one tiny microscopic portion of that life, himself so sure to share the common fate, was able to look up at the stars, to speculate upon them as he saw them through the fog that lay upon the fields. He, with his puny brain, could in some fashion comprehend the whole.

It surprised him that the police car had turned, somewhere up the road, and was coming back. Its pace was still the somewhat slow one with which it had passed him in the first place. Perhaps they were looking for someone. He wondered who.

He looked up at the stars again, and was about to begin again his speculation on them, when he noticed that the police car had stopped just before it reached him. It was stopped, and he was walking up towards it. And it was quite impossible for his lonely mind to speculate on the stars when there was some other person present. Instead, he was forced to look at the car, the black saloon with the Police notice illuminated on the front of the roof, its lights burning—though the headlamps were switched off before they tended to blind him—and the suggestion of unseen persons, heavy silent men probably, sitting behind the windscreen that was barely a glimmer in the translucent fog.

He did not cross the road to avoid the police. There was some restriction on his conduct there. Police methods were not something he had studied, but they must include, he knew, the careful observation of anything they might regard as at all suspicious. It was surprising how he, because he was intelligent and in some peculiar manner sensitive, found it necessary to behave with a quite artificial, a kind of acted correctness, in even the most superficial contact with the police. He walked straight up to the car, neither increasing his pace nor slackening it, and was going straight past it at a distance of three feet on the driver's side, when a voice from the dark interior said: "Just a minute."

He stopped. He looked with surprise into the dark opacity. He was not, for an instant, sure whether he had been spoken to or not. It might have been some private conversation between the two dim figures on the seat. He was about to move away again, into the darkness and the night, when the same voice said: "Have you seen anyone running past here?"

He moved to the car, and put his hand on the door, on the ledge of the open window. He could see the uniformed figure at the wheel then, and the second just beside him. His curiosity was aroused. Someone running? He connected the question with the scream.

"No," he said. He was aware that he had paused rather lengthily before replying. That had been because he had not known whether to address the driver as "Constable" which might be too little, or "Officer", which would probably be too much. Both methods of address had seemed to him artificial for the strange stillness, and indeed intimacy, of the fog-bound night in the country lane.

"No," he said. "I haven't seen anyone this way except myself."

He was answered by a silence. So far as he could see, the two men were not looking at him at all, but forward, through their windscreen, along the lane. He paused irresolutely. He wondered if, as an ordinary citizen, he should ask them what they wanted. Or whether their silence was itself expressive and indicated that he had been dismissed. He rather thought the latter, that the conversation had been concluded and that it was not his business. He was on the very point of moving away again.

"Would you mind, Sir," the second man said, the one beyond the driver, "coming with us just a minute?"

"Mind?" said Clem. He wondered what it was, that he was finding himself involved in. Yet he felt an odd sense of pleasure, that he had been singled out in some way to help. "I don't mind," he said. "It's only that I wanted to be back at my hotel by midnight."

They did not answer that. They were indeed a silent pair. The driver reached back and opened the door for him, with the obvious intention that he should climb into the back seat. There was a strange dichotomy, he noticed, between their slowness of speech and the speed with which, no sooner was he in the car, and before the door was properly closed, the driver let in the clutch and began to drive away.

They were going back over the route he had just traversed. He felt a shade of resentment then. So he was going back to the woman who had screamed, after all. It had proved futile for him to walk away. Yet there had been enough people there, he was sure of that. Why then did they want him? The question was only in his mind for an instant, when the sergeant —it was a sergeant by the driver—asked:

"And which hotel is that?"

He had all but forgotten that he had said anything about getting back to his hotel. It took him a second to follow the sergeant's remark at all. Then he told them, promptly.

In the ensuing silence as the car went at a steady pace along the road, he realised that he was probably giving every appearance of self-contradiction. He wondered if it was that they were thinking about, the two dark heads that were before him: the fact that he was, by his own account, going back to his hotel by what was probably the wrong direction and what was certainly not the shortest route. But surely, he thought, if they did wonder, they would ask him why. After all, he only had to tell them that he had been going for a walk. It was the fact that they did not ask, although they had interested themselves in him, which worried him.

"I'm a stranger here," he suddenly volunteered. "My name is Harold Clemens. I'm an industrial chemist. I've been visiting the factory today and I will again tomorrow. I came out for a walk."

No answer. Not even the slightest move from either of the heads. He began to wonder if the police as a whole were obtuse, or just ill mannered. Or were they wondering why he had found it necessary to explain himself?

"I was hoping to get back to the town by this lane," he said. "I thought I ought to be able to turn right again and get to the town centre. Could I? For future reference?"

He was making a definite, indeed a quite frightened effort to communicate with them. His alarm arose from the fact that the conversation seemed to have become one sided, as though he had had no need to speak at all, but, having spoken, was bound to go on explaining himself, to iron out the kinks.

After an appreciable pause, it was the driver who spoke. He said : "Three miles."

There was something so uncompromising about the brevity of that reply that Clem subsided into his seat in a state of wonder. He must remember, if ever he were arrested, he thought, not to talk at all. As it was, he would have tried again, impelled, in some strange fashion, despite himself. But he saw that they were already passing the junction

14

of the street he had emerged from onto the lane. They must be at their destination.

The houses of the suburb, having appeared, had stopped again. It was down a short, but dark and wooded lane that the car turned. It drew up in front of an isolated modern house.

"Just come with us, if you will, for a moment, Sir," the sergeant said, opening his door. "I don't expect we'll keep you for a minute."

His tone was so easy that Clem felt that the panic, the peculiar sub-panic, that he had been getting into in the car, had been quite unjustified. He felt greatly reassured, though somewhat puzzled. He had no idea what part of police procedure it was to pick up someone from the road and take him to a house. His objective interest in what was happening was greatly intensified by the sight of an ambulance turning into the street from the other end and drawing up outside the gate of the house as they went inside.

They were in a lighted hall, an ordinary, better-class, suburban villa hall. For a moment he was left alone there. The driver had gone out to speak to the ambulance men, and the sergeant had asked him to wait while he himself had gone on into a lighted and apparently crowded downstairs room from which came a buzzing sound of voices talking in low tones.

The driver was standing at the gate talking to the ambulance men and looking back at him as he stood in the hall underneath the lights.

"Right," said the sergeant, emerging from the room again. "You can come in, now, Sir. Try not to disturb her. She's suffering from shock, but fairly clear what happened."

It dawned on Clem, in some inexplicable fashion,

15

that whatever had happened had happened in the street. He seemed to sense it even before he saw the woman lying on the couch, the lady of the house in a dressing-gown, and the man with an overcoat over his pyjamas. There was something in the very stance of the three or four other people who were present that placed them as neighbours, as people who were simply standing round some central drama.

The peculiarity of this impression was reinforced by the fact that although the sergeant preceded him into the room no one at all of those present followed the bigger man with their eyes. They all looked past him, with a strange coldness and hunger, at the doorway through which Clem came.

For an instant he could not see the woman on the couch, and she could not see him. Then the sergeant stepped aside.

She was in a bad way. A grey-faced, thin woman who seemed surprisingly to be hardly more than thirty, she was lying in a state of nervous prostration, her head propped up but a little trickle of saliva visible at the corner of her mouth. It was with an incredible slowness, totally unlike the attitude of everyone else in the room, that she turned her eyes from the sergeant and to him.

She looked at him steadily, out of blank grey eyes. He wondered if she could see at all. It was most astonishing, and unique in his experience, to see a glance behind which intelligence was temporarily dead. And yet she must be seeing him. She stared with a kind of fascination. And then her lips crumpled in a grimace of horror, as though he were some vision, some dreadful ghost.

She said: "Yes!" She quickly turned her head away.

Clem, mystified, intercepted a glance between the sergeant and the owner of the house. It was a supremely worried glance. One of the standing women had rushed to the couch and was applying a handkerchief to the turned-away face. Behind Clem, in the doorway, were the ambulance men with a stretcher.

"Miss," said the sergeant. His tone was pleading. It was impossible to say who he was pleading with, the inert body on the couch, with its head turned away from him, or the woman kneeling beside it who had turned and was looking at both of them with a glance of near hatred.

"Miss," the sergeant said again. "Look at him and be quite sure."

A man who was standing by, a doctor presumably, moved forward to intervene. Clem found himself noticing things about the room: the inevitable radio in the corner, the polished sideboard, the unoccupied chairs and the standing people.

"She is sure," the kneeling woman said. She looked at Clem suddenly with a glance of pure spite. "You saw her look at him, and you heard her say it."

"I say!" said Clem, suddenly aware of an incipient disaster that was quite ridiculous. "Look! I don't understand. I was just walking down the street, and then—"

The sergeant was looking at him now. The sergeant said: "It's my duty to caution you that anything you say may be taken down and used in evidence."

"But this is absurd!" said Clem. It was so obvious to him that there had been a mistake that he did not know where to begin. He could imagine himself saying all the phrases from all the crime novels he had ever read. He wanted to laugh, and he actually did laugh, shortly: a laugh that was cut off abruptly as the woman on the couch gave a convulsive heave and said: "Leave me alone! Leave me alone! Take him away." Then she too began to laugh, quite hysterically.

The kneeling woman tried to deal with her. "With creatures like you about," she said to Clem, "we aren't safe outside our own front doors."

The doctor had signalled to the ambulance men that they were needed after all. They were coming in and Clem was being taken out into the hall again. All the doors were open, and the lights were shining out onto the fog and windless stillness of the peaceful night.

# CHAPTER TWO

**D**URING his trial, Clem was incredulous of the serious view which everyone took, including his own counsel, of his situation. From the dock, and looking down at his counsel, he remembered the countless times he had told the man that the whole thing was just a silly mistake, the kind of episode that could be cleared up in five minutes if only everyone —he, the police, the woman and whoever else might be interested—could just simply sit down in a room together and talk about it quietly.

But that, he saw with incredulity, was not how justice worked. They were not sitting down in a room to talk about it. They were in court, and he was in the dock, "the prisoner," with all the effect that those words had on everyone's mind, and it was not a matter of quiet explanation and persuasion, but something theatrical, it seemed to him, as though the affair were a melodrama taking place on the stage.

"Now, Miss Smith," the prosecuting counsel said. "I want you to look carefully at the accused. Can you honestly, and without any shadow of doubt, tell us that this is the man you saw at the moment that you screamed?"

It was there again, "the accused." As Clem turned to face the woman, to meet her eye if only she would meet his, which she had positively refused to do since the trial started, he thought how different it would be if, instead of having him produced for her by the police, he had simply met her in the street, or been introduced to her as "Harold Clemens, usually known as Clem, one of the men who make those plastic gadgets you find so useful in the kitchen". But it was not like that.

She did look at him. But he felt even then that she was looking at him without seeing him. She was seeing the dock perhaps, or the situation as a whole, the appurtenances and the procedure of the court. Or, if she did see him, it was surely in relation to the policeman, his sponsor as it were, who sat nearby.

"Yes . . ."

Her response was only semi-audible.

She was a thin, wasted-looking woman, who, he had learned without astonishment, was only thirty. She had a frail, mousy appearance, as though her clothes, not only the coat and the quite pathetic hat she wore in court, but all her clothes, had been chosen solely with the view of escaping attention so far as possible. Her very pathos, the faded gentility of her manner, which could not really be a faded anything but only something she had learned, had all worked against him. She was an archetype, surely, the very essence of what was meant by a "lady", in the sense of that fragile feminity of a past age which had to be protected from marauding men. And after she had appeared to look at him, she did look, actually and pleadingly, at the judge, as though asking him how long, how much longer, this torture must go on.

To Clem, she was utterly and completely incredible. From his position in the dock, he could only look at her with an appalled amazement.

His experience of women was by no means vast. Yet he had worked with women. He had talked with women, young and old, on a variety of subjects. There were a few women who, in the course of his work, he had met day in, day out, year after year. He had not formed a high opinion of their intelligence. On matters such as politics they had seemed to him to rely too much on their own personal experience, of shopping and of the appearance of successful men on the one hand and "the workers" on the other. They had not, he felt, an adequate grasp of abstractions or the broader issues. But this, this woman in the witness stand, was something outside his experience altogether.

Even now, as she looked pleadingly at the judge, and answered her counsel's further questions, to which he did not listen, it was so patently obvious, to him at least, that it was herself she was thinking of. She was totally preoccupied with her own position in the witness stand, with the things she had to say and do, with the awful, awful experience of having to tell what she had endured—or dreamed.

The words of his counsel came back to Clem:

"In a certain proportion of these cases, Clemens, the supposed attack proves not to have taken place at all. But in this kind of case—and I'm afraid yours is one —the burden of defence is most difficult of all. After all, if she sticks to her story that some man did attack her, and then turned right along the lane, then it follows that since you were in the lane at the time, and the only person in the lane at the time, then you must either have seen the man, or you must have been him. If I had been able to warn you from the very moment you were picked up by the police, I would certainly have said: leave yourself a loophole. Tell them that you did hear a rustling somewhere along the hedges or that you thought you saw a figure in a field. But it is too late for that now. It is not that I would fail to advise you to lie your way out of this, but that the chance is gone, in fact, from the moment that the accused makes his initial statement to the police."

Counsel had seemed incredibly cynical to Clem. He had even wondered if his solicitors had not made a mistake, if they should not have chosen a man with a higher sense of professional ethics, someone who by his probity and integrity, his obvious inability ever to countenance any lie, would have made a better impression on the judge and jury. It was only in the face of the *fact* of Miss Emma Smith in court that Clem began to realise that not merely was human justice only human, but that anything that Emma Smith said was likely to be treated as the truth not only by the jury but by all the public in the court, while anything he said would be treated automatically as a lie. The unspoken assumption of the court was precisely that of his counsel: that he would, quite automatically, and without any real implication of moral blame, say exactly whatever he could say, true or not, that would get him out of the danger in which he found himself.

The medical evidence had already come and gone. The woman had been suffering from shock—or, yes, just possibly, halucination. She had been bruised— yes, it was just possible that her bruises had been occasioned when she had fallen to the ground. Then there had been the other evidence, which Clem had been shocked to hear talked about in open court until he had realised that they were falling over backwards not to do more damage to the susceptibilities of Miss Emma Smith, or her reputation, than could possibly be helped. It had amounted to a couple of phrases from the doctor. Yes, it was possible that the more intimate injuries had been self-inflicted. But not, of course, by a woman who was sane.

The court recessed for lunch. It was generally hoped that the case might be concluded in the afternoon.

Clem himself had not yet realised that that one word "sane", which had only been mentioned once, was in fact the essence and the hinge upon which the whole case turned. All he had done was to grasp the fact that if Miss Smith had in fact been attacked, then the prosecution had made a watertight case against him, hingeing partly on the circumstantial evidence of his position at the time but ultimately on the woman's word.

It was on the latter point that he used his own intelligence and inflicted his views on his counsel when he had the chance to see him in the room below the court.

"Look," he said, "we must, we simply must get this across. She didn't recognise me, she couldn't possibly have recognised me on the night of the crime."

He paused for a fraction of an instant wondering if even his own use of words was not now being dictated by the jargon, the totally presumptive jargon, which like a net surrounded him. He plunged on desperately.

"She was in no condition to recognise anyone. The police had no business to take me in to confront her then. I'm sure you can make a stronger legal point of that. Because, although she couldn't recognise me, she could in some way *see* me. She could see me enough to recognise me again on the next occasion when they lined us up against a wall and had her pick me out. Don't you see? What I'm trying to get at more and more is the nature of her state of mind."

"I certainly do understand what you say," Counsel said. "And I'll certainly try to use it."

It was only when they were back in the court, amid the routine of the procedure, itself dulling to the faculties and reducing everything to a formal level, that Clem realised how evanescent his new point was. Seeing the counsels and the judge, and the stolid, practical, receptive faces of the jury, he realised how impossible it was for his counsel ever to put across convincingly the state of mind of a woman who was conscious enough to see but not to recognise. Opposing Counsel would have torn him to pieces in two minutes. It was not the particular, but the general state of mind of Emma Smith which was in question : a woman who was not merely accepted as normal by all around her, but who actually worked, as a school teacher as it happened, and who was not thought to be particularly good at her work, which might have rendered her open to the charge of "brilliance" with all its dangers, but who was certainly not particularly bad at it either. You could not, he realised belatedly what his counsel had realised in the first place—you could not seriously challenge the sanity of a person who day after day, year in, year out, taught classes of thirty young children and not merely kept them in order but had some success with them. Such a person, in the minds of the jurors at least, could not conceivably be described as a lunatic.

And, he realised with horror as Counsel for the Prosecution began his summing up, it was not Emma Smith's state of mind which was in question. It was his own. The counsel used the actual words, "the state of mind," and applied them to himself.

"What we have to consider, ladies and gentlemen of the jury is the mentality of a young man—and a rather solitary and somewhat abnormal young man, as I hope I have shown—alone in a strange town and wandering the streets at midnight."

Clem was appalled. He could not believe his ears. Had he been shown to be abnormal? In what way? Surely the witnesses to his sober, industrious character had not had that effect! But what a sentence, he thought in panic, what a tone-setting, question-begging outline of the survey of the case to come!

But the counsel for the prosecution held the floor firmly in his wig and gown. He was one of those men whose very presence makes the wildest abstractions solid. When he said "solitary" it was not an inference, an abstract of the vague and unrelated facts that had been revealed by witnesses. It was something that the jury could apply to their own experience, as though they too were in the habit of dividing up the circle of their acquaintances, and separating the gregarious good fellows from the lonely kind, and seeing that there was something unfortunate, and above all something "wrong" with the latter. Yet no one, Clem saw, had the slightest understanding of his method. Who would see it except someone who was himself a lonely intellectual, and of the "solitary" kind himself? Clem doubted if even his own counsel, or the judge himself, could penetrate the solid surface of the words.

"It is not a savoury subject, ladies and gentlemen of the jury," Counsel was saying. "But then this is not a savoury case. It is our misfortune to have to consider it, and to understand something that is so far below our normal mentality as is the mind of that type of person whose reaction to solitude and privacy is to inscribe those obscene drawings we see on lavatory walls."

"I object!" Clem's counsel said, while Clem himself was shattered by the diabolical ingenuity of this vision. "I cannot have activities of that nature spoken of in relation to my client."

"I was not suggesting such activities in connection with my friend's client, my Lord," Prosecuting Counsel said imperturbably. "Indeed no one knows who is responsible for the decline in public morality which the prevalence of such practices indicates. All I was doing was illustrating the unsavoury nature of a case that goes indeed far beyond mere idle obscenity for its own sake."

The judge ordered the offending words to be expunged. Clem could see the atmosphere being created. The court was doing its utmost to be scrupulously fair to a prisoner whom everyone already knew to be guilty. Yet what could Defence Counsel do? Allow the words to pass unchecked, knowing that something worse would be said until he had to object and the prosecutor created the atmosphere that he wanted? There was already a sense of horror in Clem's mind, a sense of being caught up in a machine which must grind on, inevitably, to the very end.

"I accept your order, my Lord," the counsel said. He smiled at the jury knowingly. "Perhaps, in view of it, it would not do for me to lay too much stress on the other solitary habits of the accused, the nude pictures which his landlady tells us she objected to in his flat, or his books, the *Encyclopedia of Sexual Knowledge*, or certain of the novels on his bookshelves. We must pass on therefore, to the night in question, to the spectacle of this strange young man, friendless and solitary as he has proved to be, wandering the misty streets of a town at midnight after shunning all the normal forms of entertainment, the company of the fellow guests at his hotel, the relaxations which even a small town can afford, and even the common comfort of the cinema. Of course we are well aware that he had been working. There were reasons, no doubt, why he chose to take his walk not when the weather was better and the streets were still light, but at a late hour when the proprietor of the hotel himself had assumed that he had gone to bed, when the fog had closed down, and when whatever joys or company he might find in the deserted streets in the course of what proved to be a quite extensive journey—and not by any means the mere 'stepping out for a breath of air' as my learned friend here has described it—when the only company he could expect to find, ladies and gentlemen of the jury, would be lonely women, a passing taxi bearing home a late-night party, and other skulkers such as himself."

Clem knew it was the end. He knew it long before the counsel for the prosecution had concluded the first paragraph of his rounded periods. He knew it from the moment that his pictures—a Matisse and a Lautrec at which he rarely looked—had been described as "nudes", and the word allowed to pass. They were nudes. The word was strictly accurate, like everything else the counsel said, but heavily coloured.

The rest of the trial, he knew, after once having heard the kind of thing the prosecuting counsel said, would be a mere formality. The prosecuting counsel had turned the tables. He had made the state of mind of Miss Emma Smith seem far less interesting, and therefore any consideration of it far less effective, than the assumptions, however wild they were, about his own.

But Clem was not looking at the counsel for the prosecution. He no longer heard the words, the formalities which were condemning him. It was even irrelevant to him that two of the largest national newspapers were at that time running "campaigns" against sex criminals and the type of men who attacked lonely women, so that the sentence, if there was a sentence, would be exceptionally heavy or even savage.

Instead, he looked continuously at a single lonely figure, a slim woman, grey-faced and faded before her time, a woman who apparently lived a normal life, and who now sat among the public in the court pressing a small lace handkerchief to her lips.

In truth he saw only her, the woman who had identified him and already condemned him, long before the conclusion of the case.

# CHAPTER THREE

IT was five years and three months and eleven days
later that Clem, known peculiarly in certain quarters as The Clam, stood on the corner of Bairstowe
Street in the town of Hapton. He had a cosh up his
sleeve and his gaze was fixed apparently on the
contents of the haberdasher's window into which he
gazed. In fact he was watching a reflection in the
glass: the reflection of the entrance to the bank on
the other side of Lamp Street.

A car was parked against the kerb ten yards away
from him. Clem was careful not to establish too great
a connection between himself and the car. The
Harvard gang had been defeated on one occasion because a bank cashier had refused to pass between
a standing man and a waiting car. But that car had
had men in it, and its engine had been running, while
Clem's car was silent, idle and innocent, with its door
closed.

It was also just possible that the car might be
recognised and picked up at any moment, but Clem
did not think it likely. He had acquired it from a
parking lot a quarter of a mile away only after assuring
himself by observation over a week that it normally
remained in the lot from nine in the morning until
six at night. Lack of thoroughness and initial preparation was the third largest cause, by his analysis,
which had brought his fellow convicts into the gaol.

He tensed. The door of the bank was opening. A young woman emerged and turned left as she reached the pavement. She went away from him down the street. He relaxed again. He occupied himself by examining, in the laterally reversed image in the window, the position of all the pedestrians in the street. It was not yet possible to forecast exactly what their movements would be at the moment of crisis, but it was important that when the time came he should have the picture of their whereabouts etched sharply on his mind.

The second car, the one that was also standing idle, parked in a side street half a mile away, on the far side of the bank, away from Bairstowe Street, had a door that locked. With his left hand he pressed the pocket where he kept the keys that fitted. He had them ready, and furthermore he had not had to move the car or arouse suspicion in any way. He had chosen it precisely for the regularity and certainty of its position and the knowledge that he could operate it instantly and that its owner worked in an office no less than two hundred yards from where he left it.

A truck was turning out of Lamp Street into Bairstowe Street. Clem tensed again. If the cashier for Haplans Ltd., for whom he was waiting but who did not yet know that he had a date with him, were to emerge from the bank at just that moment, he would have to let him go. Very little traffic used Bairstowe Street, which was narrow, but he could not risk having a heavy truck ahead of him. The truck moved on and passed the first of the intersecting roads. Clem resumed his vigil.

He was pleased by his lack of nerves. The steady tension and excitement was just what he had expected and just what he needed to key him up. That was training. Five years of watching the warder approach and keeping the cigarette tucked in behind the half cupped hand. Five years of looking straight forward and even under observation talking without a single movement of the lips. It was habit. He knew exactly what they could do to him, and he knew that he could face it. Neither trials nor gaols had any terrors for him, he had seen both. He knew the police and he knew their methods. He had heard a hundred stories, retailed with analytic detail, of operations such as this. And he had forgotten nothing.

He moved only a little to look at his watch. By his estimate there was less than a minute to go. He had been standing in his "ready" position for only two minutes so far. The average time the cashier took in the bank was eight minutes. Clem had not taken up his post until the man had had five minutes in there. He had been safe in assuming that the cashier would not come out in less than five or more than ten minutes. Until the last few seconds he had been prepared to abandon his post by the haberdasher's window if any pedestrian had shown any signs of looking closely at him or stopping near him. Now he was tied to it, and to everyone in the street it must appear that he had only just arrived.

You could get away with anything provided you were alone, intelligent, daring, thorough, and provided you only did it once. That was what he had learned in five years.

The first, the greatest cause of failure, of a return to prison, was eliminated by his empty car. The police derived most of their information from the lesser members of the gangs. Only one man had to appear, suddenly flush with money, in his usual haunts, or for that matter disappear from his haunts and turn up recklessly wealthy somewhere else, and the machine began to grind. The apparatus of informers, of gossip, of men who kept in touch and who could not resist the temptation to use or display a wad: all that lay in wait for the man who employed others or even told them about his latest job. It was wrong to imagine that the average criminal wanted money for its own sake. He wanted success, success in a private war against society, and that success was nothing if he could not communicate it to his friends.

Clem, The Clam, was employing two cars. He had told no one what he was doing. He would tell no one afterwards. His arrangements were as elaborate as his actions were simple. Without telling anyone who or what he was, not even the man who was to provide the alibi he would never need, he had arranged to prove that he was a hundred and fifty miles away from the coming crime.

Without appearing to do so, he kept his face turned away from a pedestrian as she passed. He turned slowly to look at another part of the window, keeping his back to her all the time. He was wearing nothing to cover his face, and his coat collar was only turned partly up. What would she remember, afterwards, when they questioned her? The raincoat and the hat.

The second greatest cause of failure was the need to repeat a job. A successful pattern, once established, was an incalculable temptation for the future. If he had ever robbed a cashier before, or if he ever had need to do so again, he would still have played the lone hand and used two local cars. The police would know instantly who had done the second job. They would know everything about him except his name. They might even know his name. They would begin to look for someone who was known by some such alias as The Clam. But not with one crime. The Clam, they knew, was a sex criminal, not a bank robber. The police rightly assumed that the leopard could not change his spots.

Standing on the corner of Bairstowe Street, with his watch ticking off the last ten seconds to zero hour, Clem mused with a new inner, high-pitched excitement, on the certainty, as he saw it, that because he had been innocent of his first crime he was going to get away with his second. That, the fact that the police did not know him in the slightest, though they thought they did, was the one thing they could not allow for.

The watch reached the minute. Clem no longer looked at it. He watched the door of the bank with the whole of his attention for five seconds, then examined the position of every pedestrian in the street for five, then looked at the bank again.

There were no thoughts whatever in his conscious mind. There was only the certainty that when the man did appear he would be carrying a brief case containing approximately nine thousand pounds in notes of small denominations and loose silver. The sum was a critical one. If it had been less, it would not have been worth a once-only chance. If it had been more, the man would certainly have had an escort and perhaps even have used a car to cover the distance from the bank to Haplans, which was only a hundred yards along the road.

The bank door opened. Immediately, Clem shifted his position slightly to the one from which the inefficient mirror of the glass gave a better view.

He recognised the grey head, the dark suit, the briefcase attached to the wrist by the short, thin chain. It was the one moment of chance in the whole business. As the cashier stepped out of the bank he might turn right or left. He had done so twice out of the five times that Clem had watched him make the journey. Twice out of the five times he had varied his route for a longer way of reaching his company's offices. He had done so last time. By the law of averages he should this time come straight down Bairstowe Street . . .

Despite himself, Clem breathed quickly in. The dark-suited cashier was coming straight across the road towards him.

Clem stood very still, watching the reflection in the glass. He knew with certainty that if he merely turned and looked at the man he would cross Bairstowe Street as well as Lamp Street and walk on the other side.

There was an elderly woman thirty yards up Bairstowe Street and coming straight towards him. There was a stout little man with a newspaper and an umbrella on Lamp Street. They were the only dangers. In the crisis of the moment Clem might have forgotten to look for them, but he had trained himself too well. His actions were going forward now despite himself, with the precision of a machine.

The cashier had crossed the road and was mounting the pavement. Clem's right arm was hidden from him by his body. Clem let the cosh slide out of his sleeve. The woman thirty yards away might have seen, but she had split seconds only and probably was short-sighted.

The cashier walked past Clem, behind his back, even then not brushing him but standing away, on the edge of the pavement, towards the conspicuously empty car. Clem turned.

The precise movements of his hands and arms had been practiced until they were quite perfect. But a slight variation had to be introduced at that point. He had been expecting the cashier to be wearing a hat, as he usually did. Clem's left hand should have knocked the hat off just before he brought the cosh down with his right hand. As it was, his left hand had nothing to do. The change of plan caused an instant's delay as Clem took up a new position and brought the cosh down.

He had taken no risk of murder. The cosh was encased in rubber. The experts in Dartmoor had told him that it would take a man of almost superhuman strength to kill a person with a normal skull with such a cosh.

It was a scientific blow, on the side of the head as he had intended. The cashier sagged rather than fell. He actually remained on his feet for a moment, being merely stunned.

Clem shouldered him roughly. It was not a nice thing, but it was essential. Within one second the man had to be lying on the ground, on his right side, with the brief case, still under his left arm, on top.

It took one and a quarter seconds, and at one point five seconds the woman began to scream.

Clem was down on one knee. He had carefully laid down the cosh beside the groaning body. He did not have to think about that. In advance, he had polished it carefully and only handled it with gloved hands. It was with his gloved hand again that he took out a pair of polished wire-cutters from the pocket of the raincoat and quickly snipped the chain.

The wire-cutters he laid beside the cosh. During the ticking milli-seconds he did not have to reason why he did that. He had arranged in advance that he should not be able to trip over either article. At two point seven-five seconds, rather longer than he had expected, he was on his feet with the briefcase in his hands. In the very act of rising, but not before, he had pulled a scarf up from under his coat and across his face. The instantaneous vision of the onlookers would not have begun to operate until that moment. Their first true glimpse of his features, their first realisation that they should look at them, would come at the moment that he covered the five yards to the car.

In three seconds flat his hand was reaching out for the car door. It was on the second stop and it opened at a touch. He put the brief case, but was careful not to fling it, on the seat. Time was precious now, but it would be just as precious later. His estimate was a whole ten minutes, during which every fraction of a second counted. He slipped into the driving seat which was the side of the car against the kerb.

It was at that instant that he saw that the woman was screaming and standing where she was, clutching her handbag and her shopping bag as though expecting him to snatch them. The stout little man could be seen in the driving mirror running straight towards him: the sort of citizen who would certainly have been murdered had Clem been a murderer with a gun. Farther down, and on the other side of Lamp Street, two men were turned towards him and one was running. The bank door was open and someone was standing there. That would be the man who would stand where he was and take the number of the car. He was near a telephone too. Clem closed the door.

He touched the starter and the engine whirred and stopped. He was as near to panic as he ever was in that particular instant. The car had started five times out of five when he had brought it to its position.

The tubby man was visible now through the window. He had bent over the cashier for an instant but now was turning to the car. The glass window of the door was up, but he waved his umbrella at it. In just a moment he would turn the umbrella end for end and use the heavy handle to break the glass. The tubby man, whom probably no one ever looked at twice, was a one hundred per cent effective citizen.

Clem touched the starter again, his left hand feeling for a second time for the ignition switch. The engine fired. The temptation was almost irresistible to race the engine and fly away with a crash of gears that would place a hopeless burden on the transmission and perhaps stop the cold engine. Clem let in the clutch slowly and drew away with a kind of quiet inevitability from the stout man who tried to catch at the handle of the door, realising just a third of a second too late what he could have done.

Clem did not accelerate swiftly. He was driving now in the middle of the road, in bottom gear. He saw his surroundings with exceptional clarity. The woman had cowered against the wall as though she expected him to chase her with the car onto the pavement. Two men were running farther up the road, and one of them was running towards a car.

He turned sharp left at the first cross road, after covering only fifty yards. He kept to his own side of the road now and accelerated through the gears to third, steadily and unobtrusively. Already he was out of Bairstowe Street and among people who had not seen the incident.

He turned sharp left again, then right when he entered Lamp Street. He was in the same street as the bank, but moving away from it. He presumed that someone would have traced his movements from Bairstowe Street, but he could not know. Behind him, in the mirror, he believed he could detect a general movement of people out of Lamp Street into Bairstowe Street. He turned sharp left again. It had not been bravado that had made him appear again in Lamp Street. He was altering course deliberately at every second block. A direct pursuit would shoot past him every time. A pursuit depending on information from pedestrians would have to stop at every corner and must necessarily be left behind. A minor cause of the number of bank robbers who arrived in Dartmoor was their habit of driving fast cars at high speed. A carefully planned route, avoiding heavy traffic and traffic lights, was better every time.

Not until he reached the main highway westwards, heading out of town, did he travel in a straight line. Then he covered six blocks at a comparatively high speed, enough to cause the pedestrians to remark him. As the road bore left, he slowed down abruptly. He turned sharp left again. He went round a block to render himself invisible from the main road, then began to move back towards the bank, travelling parallel with Lamp Street but almost half a mile from it. He stopped the car in a leafy square where the buildings around had the green windows of solicitors and insurance offices.

He carefully removed his hat and coat and left them in the car. He had made a special journey to

London in order to buy them. They were well-known makes and ready made, with cloth buttons which would not show fingerprints on the coat. He had wiped the hat-band of the hat before he set out, and he now wiped it again with a handkerchief that he then put carefully away in an inner pocket. It was a handkerchief that was impregnated with hair grease and clippings of hair that were darker than his own. The movements had been practiced, and they took the minimum of time.

He picked up the brief case, closed the car door, and walked away from it. He walked straight across the small park of trees, railings, bushes, and discouraged grass that occupied the centre of the square. When he went into the park he was a well-dressed man carrying a brief case. When he emerged at the other side the brief case was in a small attaché case. Visually, it was no longer possible to connect him with the crime.

He went straight to the second car. In his new guise, he knew that it was a risk for him to touch it. It would have been possible for him to merge with the crowd, with the other young men in pale grey suits and carrying brief cases or small attaché cases who worked in that area. But the second car was the finishing touch, the master-stroke, that would lead the chase away from him. He was, he guessed, at that point, between one and five minutes ahead of the police. But it would take them five minutes at least to trace his movements across the square, and longer, far longer he hoped, to establish the fact that the second car was missing and to get its number.

He got into it, used the keys he had already tried on it, and drove it steadily straight back through the centre of the town, passing within a hundred yards of the bank, to the main railway station. There he left it.

He walked through the railway station and out again, down the street to the town's bus station. There he retrieved a dark overcoat and scarf that he had planted earlier. He asked the time of the next bus to a place he had no intention of going to. He walked back up the street again and turned right to his hotel. He was wearing the dark overcoat and scarf and carrying the same attaché case as when he had left the hotel that morning, but he attracted as little attention as possible as he went back to his room.

Once in his room, he rapidly took off the light grey suit and his shoes and socks and tie. Together with his gloves, he put them in a medium-sized suitcase from which he took a blue suit with a mourning band and a black tie. Carefully dressed in the same clothes in which he had arrived at the hotel the previous day, he went down to lunch and chose a conspicuous table. After lunch, he told the manager that the funeral was over but he would not be going back to London until the following day.

He spent the afternoon and evening in separate cinemas in the centre of the town within a radius of a hundred yards of his hotel. The brief case was safely locked in the attaché case which was locked in the suitcase in his room. The brief case itself had not been opened yet. He bought a local evening paper not so much to read about his crime as to ascertain that the funeral forecast in the previous night's edition had in fact taken place.

# CHAPTER FOUR

MISS EMMA SMITH lived at that time in the town of Eventham. It was a Friday morning and she emerged from her private rooms in the Eventham Private School and Kindergarten as soon as Miss Haslam, the chief assistant mistress of the kindergarten, arrived.

"Miss Haslam!"

"Oh—Oh yes, Miss Smith?"

They met in the dim and over-furnished hall. It was not the day-students entrance but that used by the parents when they came to inquire about fees, to assure themselves about the quality and refinement of the school, and finally when they came from more distant places to entrust their daughters wholly to Miss Smith's and Miss Haslam's most exquisite care. In consequence the hall breathed refinement all the way from the chiming door-bell and the aspidistra near the doorway to the darkly-polished wardrobe at the far end in which Miss Haslam was engaged in shutting away her coat.

Miss Smith stepped off the pale grey carpet onto the parquet floor that gleamed faintly in the light of the fanlight. No longer inaudible, her footsteps made a clipping sound. Once having attracted Miss Haslam's attention she had to go to her before she spoke.

"I am afraid you will have to take the seniors with

the juniors for the first lesson as well this morning, Miss Haslam."

"Oh—Oh yes, Miss Smith." Miss Haslam gave a protective little tinkling laugh. She hung up her coat as though emphasising her agreement. "It's only that I'd prepared—the arrangement was that I was to take both classes for the second period—!" She had turned and was protesting politely, not so much in self-contradiction as admitting, belatedly, the disagreement which did in fact exist.

"I have had a bad night, Miss Haslam." Miss Smith looked at Miss Haslam with wide-eyed astonishment, registering a protest against the impertinence of fate. "I had toothache."

"Oh, Miss Smith! You poor dear!" Miss Haslam's sympathy flowed easily, too easily, as one who herself sought allies against the facts of fate.

"I am not a poor dear, Miss Haslam. I am as capable of bearing toothache as the next person. But none the less, I will not be able to take the seniors this morning before I go to my appointment with the dentist."

"Oh—Oh, I see. Yes, Miss Smith!"

Miss Emma Smith turned away and moved back across the hall. She thought that if Miss Haslam said "Oh" again, she would really have to correct her for it. And she was not willing to correct Miss Haslam that morning. Correcting Miss Haslam was a process that went on interminably, even more interminably than that of correcting the senior girls. And while it was perfectly true that Miss Smith could bear toothache as well as the next person, and was not even suffering from it at that moment, there was still a vast preoccupation in her mind connected with her visit to the dentist.

Blacket, the dentist at Popley, the nearby town, was, after all, a man. He was a handsome, competent, professional, bachelor kind of man. And Miss Smith's relationships with men were always—she believed always—careful and discriminate.

It was an exquisite pleasure, or duty rather, for she felt it as a duty rather than a pleasure, to calculate to the final detail her relationship with any man old enough to be her father. And that, despite the fact that she was the principal of Eventham Private School, still included the vast majority of the men she met.

She did not, knowingly or willingly, meet the other kind.

As Miss Smith returned to her private room she had a vision of the dentist, Mr. Blacket, in his white and shining surgery. Mr. Blacket had grey hair, and she saw him leaning towards her with that almost tender solicitous competence with which he looked after her teeth. Entering her room, Miss Smith promptly dismissed the image and closed the door behind her. It was not that she did not think favourably of Mr. Blacket, but she thought that the image, not the image itself but the fact that she should entertain it, was quite indecent.

She went at once to her mirror over the mantelpiece and began to examine her face meticulously with a view to identifying, before she removed them, all evidences of her ravaged night. It was not quite one hundred per cent true that toothache had been the reason why she could not take the senior class that morning before she caught the train. She had had a mainly sleepless night in the course of which she had suffered a minor amount of minor toothache, but the sleeplessness had preceded, not followed, the physical discomfort.

Her face looked as ravaged as her night had been. There was always a ravaged quality about her face. She had inherited its long, oval-shaped thinness like her ancestry and her money. She could do much with her face. She had to do much with it, for that was the face that a sufficient number of parents entrusted their children to. She did not in fact want another face. For her to have had to look in the mirror and see a youthful, newspaper, film-star face would have seemed as shocking to her as that she should have entertained in her mind the image of Mr. Blacket.

She went to her bathroom—her flat was self-contained and at one end of the body of the school—and washed her face for a second time with soap and cold water. She then went into her bedroom and changed and dressed as meticulously as a bride though with the frigid discretion of the eternal spinster. Though it was only a dentist she was going to, her underclothes were chosen to the same high standards of cleanliness and respectability as though she had been going for a major examination to a doctor. They always were. And when she had put on her severe dress and taken out her coat and hat the result was as spinsterish and respectable and as sterilising to any libidinous instincts as might have been imagined.

The spare hour which had been acquired by refusal to take the senior class was occupied in doing her hair and making up her face. That an hour could be spent in doing hair so neatly and unimaginatively, and in applying so little powder and such a tiny trace of lipstick would have seemed incredible to the kind of beauty expert which Miss Smith was not and did not wish to be. But it took almost as long to put on her dark coat and her plain hat which seemed to have been bought with the sole purpose of rendering her invisible rather than unnoticed in any bus queue or any conceivable gathering of men and women. It was a matter of the exact adjustment of a dun-coloured silk scarf around the neck, itself guaranteed to remain unseen by not attracting attention with a single misplaced fold.

When she was ready, there was still a quarter hour to spare. A slight but uncompromisingly unrecognised self-deception entered at that point. Miss Smith decided, since she had a quarter hour to spare, to walk to the station instead of waiting at the bus stop. She would not have admitted that she had arranged the quarter hour in order that she should have time to walk. By no stretch of credibility would she have entertained the suggestion that she did not trust the buses.

She went out into the hall and closed and locked her door behind her. Her conscience troubled her as she stood for a moment before letting herself out through the front door. Once she had not been able to slip off like this in the middle of the day, even for so official a purpose as a visit to the dentist. Once she had been an assistant mistress in a county school, and it was only the inheritance of her money which had made the difference between her present state and that. Perhaps she should have arranged a Saturday morning appointment if she could. But it was too late to do so now, and she let herself out and began to walk, with quick, mincing steps, towards the station.

# CHAPTER FIVE

HE awoke to the morning when the wintry sunlight was already touching the chimney pots and rooftops onto which his bedroom window gave him a level view. Although he had slept longer than he had intended and longer than he had imagined that he would, he lay for a moment thinking.

The police would have set up road checks when they heard of his departure in the first car. They would have renewed their vigilance, and given different orders by radio, when they heard of the theft of the second. When they had discovered the second car, they would have shifted their interest to the railways. He was fairly sure they would not have traced him through the railway station to the bus station. If they had, they would still think of him as out of town. But he was sure that they would have concentrated their attentions on the passengers leaving the main line trains to the north and south. The trail would have been so clear to the railway station, and there it would have stopped. Their natural points of search would be London and Glasgow. They might consider the possibilities that he had gone to Birmingham, Manchester, or Liverpool.

He got up and dressed and was in time for the latest breakfast. He asked the waiter the time, saying he had to catch the ten-thirty train. When he paid his bill at the cash desk they asked him if they should call a taxi. He said no. It was a pleasant morning and he had only the one light suitcase and the small attaché case. He would walk to the nearby station.

He went to the buses and kept away from the cloak room and the inquiry desk. He boarded a bus that would take him to a small town twenty miles away. In the course of the slow journey as the bus wound its way from village to village, he wondered how soon he dare open the brief case. He had carefully not done so until that moment. The money he was spending was his own money. It was true that Haplans Ltd. was a firm who employed mainly female labour, which meant that the money would be in small denominations, but he could afford to take no chances with marked notes at that, or any other, stage.

He was too confident actually to need to look at the money. He was pleased to find that he felt neither unduly acquisitive, nor had he any particular sense of guilt which might have subjected him to pointless fears. He did not, for example, have to look to discover whether he might not, with infinite elaboration, have stolen an empty brief case. He knew what he had to within the nearest thousand pounds. The exact figure was unimportant. His necessity had been simply that of any prisoner leaving gaol and facing the employment market. He had decided quite two years ago, when his sentence had still nearly half to run, that he was not going to go through the long process of accepting work from employers who only took him as a favour, of taking only such jobs as were open to those with the worst of references, and of being subjected, late in life, to the denunciation of being an ex-gaol-bird.

Perhaps that was some sign of the effect that events

had had on him, he thought as his bus neared its destination. He had now a taste for secure respectability, and a will to wish it on himself, which had been absent from his motives before his trial. Then it had been merely a matter of money, of adequate success in suitable work. Now it was something more.

The bus arrived and he and the rest of the passengers trouped out into a town that was almost exactly like the one that he had left. He had not been there before, and he was more surprised than usual at the uniformity of the pattern imposed by history and geography on human life. As he stood in the unfamiliar main street he took an ironic pleasure in noting the similarity of the people, their virtual identity with one another and with their opposite numbers in the other town. Born in different circumstances they would inevitably have been naked savages, ancient Romans, Aztecs, or bank bandits such as he. And yet he could not hope to live his future life without them. Indeed, he must not. It was in the possibility of being pushed into mental isolation, of finding comfort only in the company of those who, like himself, knew no law, that the greatest danger came.

The watery sunlight gave place to shadow as a cloud crossed the blue sky above the crowded street. He shivered slightly in a little gust of wind. The hooting, grinding traffic and the hurrying pedestrians seemed for a moment utterly alien to him. But it was not a new thing. He felt that he had always felt like that. They were not merely alien to him. They were alien to one another.

He saw the railway station at the far end of the street without having to ask. He made his way towards it, carrying his luggage. The burden irked him, and yet he knew it was essential. The police, looking for their bank bandit and car expert, would definitely not be looking for someone on foot who carried two cases. The disguise was sufficient to render him quite colourless. It placed him, in view of his careful clothes, as the younger type of inefficient salesman, of whom there were millions.

He had no reason to expect any trouble when he took a train. It was not even as though he were on the main line or making a long journey to anywhere in particular. The station only served a line that ran erratically westwards across the country. The booking clerk did not even look at him as he gave him a ticket to a station, a minor junction, four stops down the line.

On the station platform, where he was able to put his luggage down, he saw a copy of a daily paper. His robbery had made the right-hand front page column. Even that was routine. There was almost always a similar crime of some sort in that particular column of that particular paper. The readers would have been no wiser if the account had been entirely fiction instead of the normal half and half. But the editor had been right about one thing, so far as he could judge from the headlines of the paper on the bookstall. The interest of the readers was concentrated on the mechanics of the crime. While the lead story and the banner headline on a political issue were quite subjective, and implied a moral issue, the crime report was factual.

On the windy, grey platform he compared the treatment of the crime he had committed with the crime he had not. Apparently the newspaper readers were capable of admiring his ingenuity in his second effort. But the first, that savage sentence, had been born out of the outcry the newspapers were conducting against the frequency of sex crimes. Clem did not pity people, but he speculated about them until the train came in.

He had a third class ticket and he was lucky to get a corner seat in an already partly occupied third class carriage. He put his luggage on the rack and sat down and cleared a space on the already steamed-up window. A respectable man with a watch chain sat opposite to him, reading the *Daily Herald*. A woman and a child were in the far corner, a soldier on his own side, and a young woman in the middle of the opposite seat: a shy young woman, evidently, or she would have moved to occupy his corner which had been left vacant when he came in. Clem wondered who these people were who travelled so regularly on all the trains in the middle of the day. It was fortunate for him, and no doubt suited to the English sense of justice, that it was not the custom to discuss one's business.

The train pulled out, peacefully and unhastily. Trains had been faster sixty years ago, in the nineteenth century. They had given up the attempt to compete. They were a pleasant, decaying feature of life in a pleasant, decaying country. Clem had never felt so safe, so utterly at ease, in his life before. He was moving steadily away from the crime across unknown country in a place and in a fashion where no one could suspect him. He looked out of the window, which was steaming up again, at the winter landscape, at the chicken sheds and the cows. After less than ten minutes the train began to stop again, and he knew it would proceed that way, stopping and going, with no sign of haste or violent motion.

A station like the other. They had been villages once, but now they were all towns, as alike as peas. A porter trundled a barrow along the platform, but that was in connection with some other train. A man with a coat over his arm walked quickly past. A thin woman was walking towards their carriage.

Clem froze.

It was a moment of pure and incalculable horror. If it had been a police officer coming towards the carriage it would not have made half so much impression on him. He was ready for that, arrest. He thought he had accomplished the perfect crime, but it was always possible that he had made some slip. If he were arrested and sent back to gaol he was perfectly capable of being philosophic, in the real sense, about the whole thing. But this was something different, something which had been incalculable, and which therefore shattered him by its unexpectedness.

The woman was Emma Smith. And if there was any woman he remembered it was Emma Smith. She came right up to the door of the carriage. She had her hand on the handle, and then she tried to peer through the centre steamed-up window. The impression she must have received was that the carriage was already full, for she moved away. They could hear her open the next door along the train.

"There was room for her," the stout woman with the small child said, pleased that the stranger had not come in.

Clem was oblivious. He was looking out of the window fixedly, shocked by his own emotions. He certainly had not seen the woman since the trial five years ago, and he had never expected to see her again.

Had she seen him? Definitely, he imagined, no. She had betrayed no sign of recognition. She had behaved exactly as a woman looking into one carriage, seeing it to be full, and moving to the next. Why then his horror? Was he affected by the chance of her seeing him or by his sight of her?

She might see him. She might see him when they got out. His whole mind was instantly engaged with grappling with this problem. Because the train had already pulled out of the station it seemed to be urgent in the extreme.

He had three, or was it four, stops to go before he reached the junction where he would descend and take another train. That gave her ample opportunity to leave the train before he did. But he faced the appalling fact that it was most likely that she too, and the majority of the people on the train, were travelling to the junction. They were likely to meet. They were likely to meet on the platform at the junction, or, if he got out before then, then they would meet at some ticket barrier, or at some place from which he could not escape from her, in a queue.

He did not, could not, consider whether this was a reasonable proposition, nor what the chances were against it at any particular station. The fact that she had come to his train, come straight to his carriage, and then gone into the one next door, seemed to him to be itself illogical, a coincidence so much beyond the probabilities of coincidence, that mere logic, and the ordinary mathematics of chances, could not apply.

He must act. The moment he realised it he felt

another panic. He saw the danger then: that he would be forced into some panic action that would reveal him, would destroy all his careful calculations of his chances, and so prove fate, fate which to him was represented by one woman, to be inexorable. It would be not she who condemned him. It would be his own guilt. And yet it would amount to the same thing. He would prove himself to be helpless, a puppet in the hands of the gods.

It was moments, whole minutes, before the steady movement of the train, and the slow unfolding of the countryside, brought him back to sanity, to an appreciation that her presence on the train was merely an unlucky chance, and could be no more, and that a little sane and steady thought could save him from a meeting with her if that was his intention.

It was his intention. He decided that as the train rattled over a bridge and he looked down on a river. The chances against meeting her had not been so great as he had supposed. There had always been the chance that at some time during his operation, which had involved great crowds of people and several towns, he might meet someone who knew him. Given that assumption, then the chances that it might be her were no greater and no less than that it might be anyone else. It had only been some strange emotion that he had not known he had that had distorted his appreciation during the moments immediately after he had seen her.

And he had time to think. The nature of the fact that she was in the next compartment was that it gave him ample time, even before the train reached the next stop, to plan and shape his movements by the light of reason. As soon as he had decided that, he got up and took down his luggage from the rack.

The man opposite to him carefully drew his feet back, making ready for him to leave them at the next stop. The very naturalness of the movement helped to reassure Clem. There was nothing peculiar about his movements. Except in relation to one woman he was immersed in a vast anonymity no matter where he went or what he did on that particular line. Clem even felt a fierce joy: a joy as reasonless and causeless as had been his panic.

When the train drew into the next station, he had everything under control. He had the window lowered, and his hand was on the handle. Even before the train stopped he opened the door, and as soon as it was at a standstill he turned and took his cases from the floor of the carriage. He began to walk forward along the train, away from *her* compartment, and regardless of the fact that everyone else on the platform was going in the reverse direction towards the exit. He needed some reason for going the way he was, and he saw it before him, the "Gentlemen" sign. He had been prepared to step into a waiting-room, but that was better.

He turned in the entrance. He could see her getting out of her carriage, turned away from him, and immersed in the purposeful railway crowd. So his action had been needless. He could have gone on to the junction and taken no notice of her whatsoever. His panic and joy alike had been irrelevant to the actual situation but had arisen from the distant past. Yet while she was still on the platform he could not return to the train. It was better to remain where he was. His presence in the entrance to the lavatory gave him a reason for missing the local non-corridor train. He went inside the lavatory and waited there until he heard the train pull out.

He emerged onto the platform carefully. It was empty now, and brighter now that the train had gone. There was one porter with a truck and an old man sitting on a seat. With his cases in his hands he walked slowly down towards the porter.

"When's the next?" he asked.

The porter looked at him and at his luggage and grinned. If he had seen him leave the train and go into the lavatory and come out again, he was probably thinking that he had been wise to take the luggage with him instead of leaving it in the carriage and trying to beat the train.

"Another fifty minutes, Guv."

Clem turned away and went to an empty seat and sat there with his luggage. He felt reassured, by the intelligence of the porter and by the disappearance of Miss Emma Smith. The normality and returning peacefulness of everything restored his faith in life. Across the railway line he could see a row of houses, and beyond them open fields in dappled, windy sunlight. He even found it in him again to wonder why people travelled on trains in the middle of the day, but this time with special reference to the woman.

Strange, he thought, as the moments passed. Strange how powerful his emotions had been, on seeing her. Or perhaps not strange at all, but entirely natural. The porter was engaged in a long, complicated manoeuvring of three parcels and his truck.

Clem got up and approached him again, still taking his luggage with him.

"Is there a phone here" he asked. "It's the book I want, to look up a number."

The porter pointed it out to him. Clem no longer shrank from human contacts or the possibility of recognition. He realised that the vast elaboration of his plans had been on the whole superfluous. His movements after the first half hour following the crime had been sufficient to insulate him from it. He went to the phone and began to look through the book.

"Smith, Emma," he read among the many Smiths. "Eventham Private School and Kindergarten, Victoria Road, Eventham 2378."

From where he was standing at the phone he could see through the glass that surrounded him the name of the station where he was. Popley. The other name, Eventham, had been where she had got on. He slowly closed the book.

He went back to his seat and sat there, waiting for the train: waiting for it and at the same time forgetting it.

He had planned exactly the moves he would have to make to use and enjoy the money he was carrying. It had been, in his intention, a long-term business. Not for him the attempted disappearance, the change of name, the idle prosperity which anywhere, in any town or hamlet throughout the country, would draw attention to himself. Instead, there was the Plan, a rigorous re-habilitation no less, performed under the very eyes, those of the probation officer for example, to whom he was still technically supposed to report each week, of those who were set to watch him.

But in those lengthening minutes on the railway station he sank more deeply into his preoccupations and his desires. Thoughts crossed his mind: **what** would he do with his prosperity, his freedom, when he finally had it? And was there not something else, some other motive, discovered or rediscovered, the exercise of which could be combined with his plans as he had foreseen them?

Perhaps the other motive, born of two thousand nights sitting or lying but forever thinking in a cell, was in fact the more fundamental of the two. Perhaps he had always had it, since the trial. Perhaps he had carried it about with him, like some burden on his soul. But now, sitting on the seat in the railway station, he took it out and examined it.

The Clam was, after all, a creation of five years only. Already, after only weeks of freedom, that other person, called Clem or Clemens, was stirring underneath. They were two very different people. Somehow they must be reconciled. He tried to think what it was that separated them, what difference there was between the one self, at that time existing, and the other, the boy as he now thought of him, who had been.

It seemed to him that all that lay between them was a shadow: the shadow of a woman.

# CHAPTER SIX

$\mathbf{S}$HE had seen him. With her hand already reaching out for the carriage door, peering into the compartment that had drawn up opposite to her on the platform, she had seen the face through the irridescent halo of the steamed-up glass.

Standing, looking not at but beyond, held motionless by emotions that had sprung upon her suddenly from the buried but better-not-remembered past, she had hesitated in unbelief. Then she had turned, moving away deliberately, not thinking, not even believing quite. She had gone through the motions of getting in the train. She had opened another door, entered, closed it behind her, and seated herself in another part-filled carriage, sitting very still and waiting.

It was not that she was surprised to see him there. She did not involve herself in calculations, as she might have done, of dates, of the date that had been and the date it then was, and the number of the intervening years, and the period of his sentence, and the subtraction for remission. It was on another plane, the problem. It was not when or where or why he could be, but whether he could, in fact, exist.

Outside the train, in the passing countryside, she saw first the fields and then the river, thinking: something had existed. Something had caused her to leave the place where she had been, five years ago, the town of Lepley, where she had been employed by the local authority as an assistant mistress in a school. Something had caused her to change not only the location but also the fashion of her life, refusing, from a sense of nicety as much as awkwardness or fear, to apply again to some other authority elsewhere and to relive if only for moments, in the course of an interview with strangers, the reasons why she had wished to make her move.

She had used her own resources, setting up in a small way on her own, as she was quite entitled to do and as women did who had the money, not only daring to set up in opposition to a state-owned education system that was not only free but nation-wide, but succeeding, attracting children to her, the parents paying not only for something they could have had absolutely free, but believing, believing that the one who did set up on her own must therefore have something more to offer, since she demanded payment for it.

Everyone, in short, had been most kind.

She tried to bring herself to the point, to the actual consideration of him as an existant, living man in the next compartment further along the train. But was he real? Did he actually exist there, or was he just a figment of her imagination, a trick played upon her nerves by a stranger's face and the light and backlight on the steamed-up window, the double light, since it included that also which had come through the train?

During those five years at Eventham she had dismissed him, had to dismiss him, from her mind. She could not have lived, from day to day, in constant memory of that night, or even of the trial. And even before that, before she had moved to Eventham, before even the trial had taken place at all, she had closed the night off, the night of the suburb of Lepley, in a sealed compartment of her mind.

Nice people did not think about those things.

Nice people positively refused to think about them, either in detail or in the whole. At the trial, when she had had to stand up there and her counsel—the prosecuting counsel, for he was not hers, it was out of her hands—had asked her questions, she had said "Yes", and "Yes". She had let justice take its course, for what other way had there been to dispose of it, to seal off the night, to eliminate it and set it, even officially, in that past which no one with taste and discretion, and therefore no one who mattered, would ever voluntarily recall?

It was not a man who was sitting in the next compartment, close to the window and looking out through a steamed-up window. He was an abstraction rather, a principle of evil, even as he had been at the trial.

Respectable people, and school mistresses in particular, and particularly those school mistresses who set themselves above the rest and ran private schools, did not spend their time pondering the reality, the actual and physical existence, of those inhuman, sub-human, unreal and therefore untrue equivalents of humanity on a lesser plane that the police chased. The essence of the matter, the only possible attitude for the good to take, provided they were to remain good, and not to be subjected to temptation, was to deny even the possibility of evil as a thing that could be thought about at all. That always had been her attitude, and particularly at the trial.

When the train came in to her station she rose, hesitated until the man near the door realised what she wanted and opened it for her, and then got out. It did not enter her mind that she might go forward along the train and look in the other carriage. At the trial she had equally deliberately not looked at him. The idea that a woman could actually look, deliberately and even willingly at a man who had ... She walked steadily away, not even hastening, among the people on the platform.

Her appointment with the dentist was due in twenty minutes. But she had only two hundred yards to go. Once having left the station and reached the main street, she looked in the windows of the shops. She was aware of the passing time and of the object displayed before her with all the art intended to attract her. She had no patience with those school girls, and even school mistresses, and grown men, who got into a panic when faced with a visit to the dentist. The matter was dealt with by a simple refusal of the mind to contemplate. What she was conscious of, beside the passage of time and the objects in the shops behind the well-cleaned glass, was that she herself, Emma Smith, was looking at them. And Emma Smith, more than anything else, was the clothes she wore, the position she held, the extreme care she took in dressing and the faultless appearance of unnoticeable impeccability that she presented to the world. She knew, in fact, that she did not wear too much lipstick even by her own standards, and that the severity of her clothes would automatically reassure every woman and never attract the eye of any man. Those were her standards, and because she kept to them most rigidly she could face the prospect of a visit to a dentist or even that of death itself.

It was two minutes to the hour, and she walked down the corridor beside the chemist's shop and into the dentist's waiting room. She seated herself carefully, aloof from the other people who were moving about uneasily or battening their minds, with naked and shameless voracity, on the magazines. When the receptionist, a new girl, came to her, there was a cool clarity, a silent commentary on the weakness of man, in the way in which she firmly gave her name.

Not even the dentist's surgery itself, with its north light, its instruments, its chromium and its chair, could shake her. She liked Mr. Blacket. Indeed, it might have been said that she loved him, unlikely and even incredible as such an emotion might have seemed. But it was because of the emotion that she treated him with an exceptional coolness, as though, if love for her could exist at all, it could only be by the raising of human relationships to an abstract and quite etherial plane.

"The weather's a little cooler, I think, Miss Smith."

"Indeed, Mr. Blacket. I noticed there was a wind."

For niceness was never visible in what was said. It was achieved by a successive elimination of layer upon layer of meaning. The lowest orders of humanity displayed their culture simply by refusal to discuss the grossest aspects of the act of sex. At a higher level, politics and religion were excluded from discussion. At the highest level of all, on which Emma Smith took her stand, everything was eliminated, between strangers, except the weather. Not even art and literature, unimportant as those subjects were, were as safe, as free from controversy, and therefore suitable, as was the weather.

Miss Smith had once even thought of banning Ceasar's Gallic Wars from her school curriculum because she had heard, doubtless by mistake and due to a wrong approach on someone's part, that there were two opinions about its value. To Miss Smith, only that was real and right about which there were no opinions whatsoever, so that everything she said, without any possibility of question, was on the side of authority and the angels.

"Miss Smith—" She was leaning back in the chair and he had some kind of instrument in her mouth—"I fear we will have to have an extraction this time."

"I had hoped," she said, when he allowed her, "that you would be able to save the tooth."

He went on with his preparations. They did not discuss his statement. Both he and she knew that her statement was not an observation on it, but only a record of mental processes. It was he who said what had to be done, and that was true beyond all question.

"Gas," he said. "Miss Beeston!" He had turned to the attendent nurse.

Miss Smith did not like gas. She disliked gas even more than the jarring, the tearing, the noise of an extraction made without it. But she accepted gas. It was more ladylike. At least she hoped it was. Her mind was always blank on the subject of whether she struggled in the final moments of going under to gas or not. For the first time, the thought that she might not be in complete control of herself, if only for a few moments only, brought her out in a sweat of panic.

He had not given her gas before. She had started with him, Blacket the dentist at Popley, six months before. She had changed her dentist then. Before that she had been going to a man called Hargreaves at Eventham. A terrible man. He had given her gas.

The machine was alongside her almost instantaneously. The silver instrument was between her teeth ("Please bite on that"), and the rubber cup was over her mouth and nose.

"Breathe deeply," he said. "Breathe evenly." Her breathing seemed to begin to gather speed. Her heartbeats became the drum-roll of a tattoo.

She was fighting, fighting for her life. It was that man, that man five years ago, who she had always said had put one hand over her mouth and nose while he held her arms pinioned with the other. Only it was real this time. The nightmare had become a fact.

A rumble, a male voice speaking anxiously, as it were off scene.

A vacancy, a vacancy of horror. A kalaidescope of images. A boy in the playground of a school, running. A naked knee and thigh. Horror. The fact of naked human flesh, with hair.

The struggle was desperate now. It was no longer on the physical plane, but on the mental. The struggle took place in a dark and windy vacancy. At one moment it took the form of words: a statement: "the naked truth". She was shocked by the obscenity, knowing it to be the foulest language. Perhaps some newspaper had said it. The yellow press.

A street, a fog. Herself alone and quite alone. Or was she quite alone? Was she not, rather, in a dentist's chair? That, she thought with horror, with all the passionate agony of a breathed revelation: that was what he did. She saw it. She remembered now, at last. Only it was not what had happened. It was what was happening. That time and this time were one. Time was an eternal present, from her earliest childhood to the present day, and time, all time, was dominated by a single theme, an event, an event not actual but what was happening then.

A face at the steamed window of a railway carriage. Only not a face. The face was irrelevant. It could be that or any other face. The reality itself was faceless, having only a body, a limbed torso without the head.

The face at the railway carriage window was substituted by that of Mr. Blacket. By Hargreaves, the dentist at Eventham. By other men. But possessing only a single body.

Yet the struggle was actual and physical. She could feel the fierce blows raining on her, about her mouth and jaw. She tried to scream, but her jaw was somehow fixed. Her whole body therefore, it seemed was equally transfixed in a naked paralysis of sheer despair, in a bent attitude, with parted knees.

The truth, the eternal truth of that continuous present which was her life. It was a man, and of all the faces, she must settle on a single one. A voice had said to her: "Is this the man?" It was, it must be. It was all of them.

Then suddenly there was a mist clearing, a light in darkness. Through the misty area she saw a face. Because of the mist, as of steam, it ought to have been the face at the railway carriage window, but it was not.

It was Mr. Blacket.

Still surrounded by the dispersing mist, with the light behind him, he was smiling at her. He was looking dishevelled, and yet he had the cheek to smile. It was monstrous. They all were. Monstrous.

"How dare you!" she was saying, outraged, as she came round. "How dare you! How dare you! How dare you!"

She saw Blacket's face lose its smile. Something else came into his eyes. It was fear.

"Miss Beeston!" he said. She heard him say it, call the nurse from nowhere, who had probably gone out and hidden in another room.

"Wash your mouth with this," Miss Beeston said. But she had gripped Emma's hand with a clasp that made her wince.

Emma suddenly began to weep. It was hopeless, heartbreaking and frightening. There was nothing to do about it, with the female there, the nurse, the pander, to support his word.

She would have to change her dentist once again. It was bitter. It was as bitter as the salt of her bitter tears, the tears that ran down her collapsed and sagging face.

They were all the same. All men were all the same.

"Just rest," Miss Beeston said. "You'll be all right in a minute. Just rest a while."

Her voice was reassuring, or intended to be reassuring to the patient. But Emma saw the glance that passed between them, between the woman and the man. It was a glance of apprehension : and of knowledge. They were in league against her. They really were.

Miss Emma Smith had already begun to draw a veil over the incident when, quarter of an hour later, she staggered out. She was engaged in that lengthy, and in fact eternal process, of pulling herself together.

"Your course of treatment is finished, Miss Smith," Blacket had said. "Those other appointments you booked, for the next few weeks, are quite unnecessary, after all."

"Mr. Blacket is a very busy man," the nurse had said. "If you need any urgent treatment at any time, I'd really advise you to try elsewhere."

Miss Emma Smith had one thought only in her mind: to get back to the school and take up there where she had left off. It was more than a wish on her part. It was a necessity. And as for the face at the railway carriage window, she had forgotten it. It was part of her dream, her dismissed dream, which she no longer thought about: no more.

# CHAPTER SEVEN

IT was on a Thursday evening that the sergeant studied the man on the other, the public side, of the black counter in the small, clean, dingy inquiries room of the police station at Eventham. The sergeant's attitude had contained that caution, that imperturbable determination to await the other's gambit, which is the property of all deeply invested officials and which reaches its most aggressive blankness in certain branches of the police. Now it was deepening into suspicion. Outside the door and the obscured window the town's noise and traffic lights went past. The room itself was illuminated by a single naked electric bulb, giving the light that slightly obscure, grey harshness of a print from an overdeveloped photographic negative.

"You say your name," the sergeant said, "is Harold Clemens?" He stood two feet back from the counter, and the constable, who had called him and surrendered the interview to him, hovered three feet farther back again and a little to one side.

"I don't *say* it is, it is," Clem said. He smiled agreeably to palliate his correction. He must, he knew, pay the price, accept the increased suspicion that was always accorded to intelligence and the refusal to accept the implication of what to another was probably only a form of words, but the undertaking he was embarked upon was such that he must present his character to the sergeant to within one degree of the final truth.

"When did you come out?" the sergeant said. "When did you finish this term you say you served?"

"Six weeks ago," Clem said. "Look, Sergeant, I don't have to come to you. Or if I do, if I have to report at intervals, there's still no call on me to discuss my plans. It isn't incumbent on me to do anything towards that trust I'm trying to establish between us now. It's just that I want to."

"So you said," the sergeant said.

"Well," said Clem philosophically, "I can't expect you to welcome me with open arms. Like they do on the films, if you were a sheriff I expect you'd run me out of town."

At that point there was some obscure feeling moving in the sergeant. The man had not come there for nothing. There was a need, perhaps, even in the square-built Georgian police station at Eventham, and on a wet evening, to exercise guile and craft.

"I haven't said we object to your coming here," he said with an innocent openness. "You can go where you like. You're free."

"There is that," Clem said, and laughed. "Until some woman complained she had been accosted," he added. "Or someone snatched a handbag. Or someone was thought to have committed indecent exposure in front of little girls. Perhaps all those things. At each one of them I'd expect to be visited by the police, arriving in uniform, with a car parked outside my door."

"You won't have cause to fear anything if you're innocent," the sergeant somewhat sharply said.

"I've told you what I fear," Clem said. "Not conviction. Just too much contact, not between you and me, but between constables in uniform and plain-clothes detectives and all the people I may have come in contact with and who might be in a position to give you a line on me. I can't help it, I know. I'm bound to be, to begin with, anywhere, the man the police made inquiries about when he first appeared. I'm just trying to mitigate it. I'm trying to tell you the simple and obvious and actual things I intend to do, so that you won't have to make inquiries to discover those, at least."

The sergeant's suspicions had deepened, but at the same time there was an uneasiness. It was possible—hardly credible, but just possible—that a reformed lag, an ex-prisoner, might forsee the future. It was even possible, though not so likely, that, forseeing it, he might still persist, for a while at least, in trying to be that very thing, respectable, which his record and his past precluded that he should be.

"You see I'm not really a criminal type," Clem said frankly. "That's my trouble."

The sergeant wondered why he bothered to say the words: words which, even if true, he could not be expected to have believed.

He spoke cautiously, supremely cautiously, since to accept the other's gambit was to some extent to play his game, to commit himself, to admit perhaps, however indirectly or by inference, that there might be inquiries made:

"Have you some special reason for coming here?"

"None," said Clem, with exactly the same inno-cence as before. "Except that so far as I know there is no one here who knows me. I'm a hundred miles, in two directions, from where anyone will be likely to associate me with my past."

"You can't escape your past," the constable said suddenly, "by running away from it. You'd do better to face up to it."

"All right, Hargreaves," the sergeant said. He turned to Clem. "Your employer," he said. "If what you want us to do is to conceal from him the fact that you've been in gaol—if your last reference is from the Governor of Her Majesty's gaol—we can't."

"I have money," Clem said. "Not much; a little."

Both the sergeant and the constable went on looking at him. Perhaps, in their wildest dreams, they thought for a moment that he was going to try to bribe them. Clem reached into the inner pocket of his jacket and pulled out a post office savings book. He opened it and looked at a page, then bent it so that it would stay open, and put it on the counter. Neither the sergeant nor the constable touched it or moved near enough to see the figures.

"I once had a balance of a thousand pounds," Clem said. "You'll see how that was accumulated on the preceding pages: by banking the annual bonuses my employers gave me over five years. I had hopes of getting married and buying and furnishing a house someday. That big subtraction at the top of the page is five years old, the cost of the trial. The balance has been drawing compound interest ever since. I ought to have come out completely ruined and dependent on an employer who wouldn't want to employ an ex-convict anyway, but I didn't. I made three small withdrawals the last six weeks. I've still got five hundred pounds."

They still did not look at the book. They might

someday check Clem's statements, but if they did it would not be by the simple process of looking at a book which he produced.

"You want us not to subject you to the inconvenience of being suspected of snatching handbags?" the sergeant said.

Clem, standing back from the counter as much as did the sergeant, said:

"I want to buy a business."

Their dubious looks were sufficient of a question.

"That's why I'm here," Clem said. "I've been looking for a shop to buy. I've better qualifications than would lead me to the kind of shop you can buy for five hundred pounds, not the property but the goodwill and the lease, but I can't use them. I've got to set up in business on my own. And it couldn't be a second-hand dealers or anything to do with cars or metal. It had to be a back-street or a suburban grocers in a small way. And I've found what I want in Eventham."

And could have found it in any other town in the length and breadth of England, Clem thought, if he was prepared to accept, as he had been, an agent's glowing account and the absence of books for a tiny business that had been allowed to run down. But he did not say that. He was too busy watching the effect on the constable and the sergeant of the admission, at last, of what he was going to do and what it had to do with the town that was under their jurisdiction.

"Have you actually done this?" the sergeant asked, his caution again apparent, "or is it something you hope to do?"

Clem could see his mind moving by this time. He could see the sergeant facing the prospect of an old lag setting up in business in Eventham. Not a second-hand dealers or anything to do with cars or metal: he had registered that. He had already faced the possibility that Clem was going to become a fence. But that was only the surface. The main thing was that the story was now established. It was something actual in the sergeant's mind, the problems an ex-prisoner faced and the way this particular one was coping with them on his doorstep. It was not just a matter of the moment but something he was going to have to deal with in the future.

He sealed that feeling, that earnestness, that sense of reality. "I signed a document this afternoon," he said. "It was immediately after that that I came to you."

The sergeant moved. He came to the counter, picked up the post office savings book that was lying there, glanced at it for just an instant, and handed it back to Clem. Officially, he was just handing it back. In fact, his eye had rested on it long enough to register the balance.

"I don't know that I would have advised you to do that," he said. "Business is bad in Eventham." It was not only apprehension. He forsaw a future in which the ex-prisoner would fail to make good his business and so return again to crime.

And, thought Clem, you would not have advised me to do anything else in Eventham either. You would have advised me like every other sergeant in every other police station in the British Isles to stay away from your particular beat. Or you would not have advised me at all. You would have retained the attitude with which you began this interview and not believed a word I said—

"Business is bad everywhere," he said. "I had to take a chance." He accepted the proffered savings book, and restowed it in his pocket.

The sergeant was standing close against the counter now, looking down at it, and wondering with what words to dismiss him.

"If you are going to be here, we'll play square with you if you play square with us," he stolidly said.

Clem grinned again. "The fact that I've turned up here and told you all about myself and what I intend to do might be taken as some kind of indication of my intentions," he said.

"Yes," said the sergeant. "I appreciate that."

It was a safe concession, and yet, for once, he sounded as though he meant it.

"No turning up at my shop with uniforms in a car to question me about every crime that's committed in this district?" Clem chaffed him.

"No." The sergeant, making the best of it, permitted himself a smile. "We'll have you handcuffed and brought to us at the station."

"You'll know what to tell the banks and the local wholesalers when I want credit on the security of the stock that's on my shelves," Clem said.

The sergeant looked scared, indignant.

Clem laughed. "Goodnight!" he said. He turned to go.

# CHAPTER EIGHT

THE sergeant, whose name was Huntley, and who had a wife and two almost grown-up children, and who was within three years of the retiring age, was more than aware of Clem. News of Clem began to come back to him, almost immediately, through many contacts, most of them unofficial.

At times, on certain nights, the sergeant stood in doorways in the main street of Eventham. His very age, his experience, and the length of time he had been in the town gave point and purpose to his doing this. Late night pedestrians, hurrying along the street, would see his tall figure suddenly as they passed the doorway of a shop, hidden and shadowed, the rain hardly damp or giving a sheen to his coat or cape as though he had not, as they presumed he must do, patrolled a beat, or tried the doors, or walked the full length of the shuttered shops, but merely emerged from the police station or his home, walked to that one place, exchanging one word perhaps with the fortuitously-met constable on the beat, and then stood there, for a time that no one measured, and then gone home again, some duty, some formal routine perhaps, accomplished.

New recruits, new constables in the force, all passed through a phase. It lasted six months, or a year in some cases unless their older colleagues disillusioned them. They were under the impression that the sergeant was set to keep a check on them. They felt, indeed, as the ordinary pedestrians did, that the sergeant was there to adduce some enormous compendium of times and places, so that his shadow was enlarged, lying not only as a symbol of law and order across the town, and protectively along the line of shops, but covering their own doings with complete awareness, noting their own movements when they were late at any given point. The sergeant, it sometimes seemed to them, was the very law of which they were the servants: law and order made substantial and yet hidden. For they were ordered to take no notice of him when they saw him stationary at his post, however obvious, even to the most unobservant crook, his presence there might be.

The sergeant stood in the doorway two nights a week, and for the most part nothing happened. Occasionally some pedestrian, passing, would look back twice at him. The hours would pass. He would go home.

Occasionally someone, seeing him there, would say "Goodnight!" More rarely still, someone would stop to talk, finding him uncommunicative and monosylabic when they sought to pass the time with him. During his boring vigil, it seemed to them, he preferred the solitude of his own thoughts.

Yet the sergeant occasionally did converse with someone still deeper in the shadow. He would be standing there as usual, still looking outward at the street, and someone else would be there, beside him or behind him. It was not always the same person. There were three or four of them who sometimes stopped for a conversation of which no one heard a word. But there was one in particular, small and thin and wearing dilapidated clothes, grey-headed, and of the sergeant's age.

This was a man who earned a precarious living, sometimes, by selling papers in the street. Some said he was also a bookie's runner. At least he had lived, for over twenty years, so much on the fringe of the law as to feel the need to sustain his position with the police.

"It's a cold night, Sergeant," he said with all the uncertainty that characterised his conversation as he stood in the shadows behind the bigger man.

The sergeant grunted, uncommunicative, monosyllabic, no more forthcoming with the man who was with him now than with any other pedestrian who might have stopped to talk to him. The only difference was that this man stayed, seeming to find warmth and comfort and company from his presence, from his immobile, upright and unbending stature, while others found something cold and distant in it.

"You know the bloke what took the shop, Serge?"

The sergeant did not even answer. He did not pry or ask for knowledge. Since he had been told no less than three times about the man, the man who had taken Mrs. Hartley's grocery shop between the terraced streets and the council house estate, and modernised it, with his own hands burning off the dun brown paint and painting the woodwork white, the man who had been himself, that once, to the police station when he first arrived, and who his informant had told him, unnecessarily since he had heard it from the man's own lips first, that he had been "inside", he did not need to answer.

"Harper's going to put the screw on him," The Squirrel said.

And that was all. No explanation and no detail. They simply stood there, together in the night, like one-time lovers almost, passive in the presence of, but not in contact with, one another. And then, when the next pedestrian passed, the smaller man, the one whose habits and whose indefatigable apparent purposelessness had earned him the appelation of The Squirrel, was simply gone.

Harper, the sergeant thought, still standing, still maintaining his vigil, although released. Harper had been inside three years ago. He would have known the man called Clemens, have recognised him. Clemens, then, was coming to the first hurdle, the first and perhaps most crucial of those steps a man must climb who wished to emerge from and make a break with crime.

On the following day the sergeant himself, in plain clothes, walked past that shop between the working-class terraced streets and the equally working-class but more respectable council house estate. The shop, and Clemens himself, since he had arrived in the town and bought a worthless goodwill and a lease worth half the value for five hundred pounds, had been under constant observation. But it was not for a constable, who could report on merely facts, to make an assessment of how a man with five hundred pounds only and his credit thin, was keeping above or falling below the danger point.

The sergeant walked through the streets and passed the shop as though by chance while heading for the council estate upon some business. He saw the white window, the gleam of white inside, three housewives in there talking, and Clemens serving. He saw what he wanted to see in the fact that the wives were themselves in there, with their shopping baskets, and had not, as in old Ma Hartley's day, merely sent their children to buy a reel of thread or a faded packet of soap flakes or some other trivial item that they had forgotten when doing their major shopping in the town.

A man still young, the sergeant thought. It would be that, and the new paint, that would have tempted them into the shop in the first place, to see, for curiosity only, the new neighbour whose premises they could invade. But how had he kept them, and made them come back again, they who had got the Woolworths habit? The answer was perhaps in that half of the window that was given up to the "remnants" stock, the old tins, slightly rusty as they were, that were marked down to half price or less. Or perhaps it was the new half of the window, the contrast so obvious and impressive, of clean fresh goods on sterile shelves at prices that were no better than competitive, but the appearance of which was tempting to appetites attuned to a rough and ready greed.

The sergeant walked on. He reached the main road through the council estate and caught the bus back to the centre of the town. He had no reason to doubt the intelligence of the man. He would succeed, just as the average bright man might, if he continued to concentrate on succeeding. But that was the point in question. Harper had probably "touched" the proprietor of the shop, and demanded a loan for old time's sake, and now, talking so that even The Squirrel could hear him of how easily he had obtained five pounds, he was about to put on the screw.

The sergeant returned to his stance in the shadowed doorway some three nights later. It was a night when it had ceased to rain and the pavements were wet and glistening. He saw a man pass him and look quickly back. The same man passed in the reverse direction a second time. At the third time of passing the footsteps hesitated as they reached the entrance.

He was there, framed and silhouetted against the light, not entering, not sliding into the shadows as The Squirrel had done, but retaining his freedom as though he, larger and more burly as he was, might still need suddenly to take recourse in flight.

"Sergeant—" The sound was a prison hiss.

"Harper?"

"You got an inside man in town, Sergeant. Bloke called Clemens. He has a shop."

So, thought the sergeant, Harper had put on the screw. He had no longer "touched" but demanded. And Clemens had not come across. The sergeant did not think of the burly shape before him. He thought of the man who had come to the police station, who had had the sense to come to the police station, anticipating, though he had no knowledge or experience to anticipate, but only the imagination and the hearsay, the situation created by some such man as Harper.

"How much did you ask him for, Harper?" the sergeant said. "How much wouldn't he give you?"

It was by the shoulders, dark against the glisten of the pavement, that the sergeant read the expression of the other man. The shoulders hunched in indignation and resentment at what the sergeant was imputing and could not know.

"Sergeant!"

The sergeant said nothing. There might be more to come. There was:

"Where did he get the money, Sergeant?"

Harper said the words, then suddenly was gone.

The sergeant waited in his alcove, thinking. He remained where he was in the darkness though he did not expect any further developments to take place that night. He calculated times and places. Harper had been "in" three years ago. He would have seen Clemens then, and known him, and known about him. He would know when he was due out, and therefore he would know how long Clemens had been out now. He would assume, quite naturally, that if Clemens had money to buy a shop at this stage, then it must have come from somewhere, not knowing of the savings book or that Clemens had always had it.

There was an adequate explanation of Harper's question, yet the sergeant still thought about it as he left his doorway and walked home with the measured tread that had become a habit through the glistening night.

Some would have said that there was something unethical about the sergeant's moves the following day. They involved an interview, in plain clothes and out of duty hours, with the manager of a bank.

In the bank manager's office, in the pleasant surroundings and clear light, the manager and the sergeant talked as what they were: old friends.

"By the way," the sergeant said. "Do you happen to know a man called Clemens?"

The manager was momentarily silent with a smile. He turned blue eyes with a curious look on the sergeant's face.

"He opened an account here."

"A big one, or five hundred and thirteen pounds transferred from a post office savings bank account?"

"You know," the manager said. "It seems you know. He sat where you are sitting now and told me about the savings bank. Is there anything I should know about this man?"

There was a little silence as they faced one another across the desk, neither giving the information that they had to give, each with-holding the item that was of primary interest to the other.

"I'm not asking you," the sergeant said. "I'm telling you. He came in here and opened an account for five hundred and thirteen pounds. He warned you at the time that he would be drawing a cheque for five hundred within the next few days. He told you about the shop he was taking and the goodwill and the stock and lease. He promised that the documents would all be handed across to you. He asked you for credit for either fifty or a hundred, or two hundred pounds."

"We don't discuss our client's business," the manager said, "but we can't prevent people guessing, even if they guess correctly. Is the exact figure of the credit at all important?"

"No," the sergeant said.

"You aren't warning me that the lower figure would be more realistic than the latter?"

"No," the sergeant said. "Let me go on guessing. My guess is this. That whatever the credit was when you granted it, the overdraught was short lived. It was not that the man Clemens ceased to owe money, but that he transferred the debt from you to the wholesalers who supply his goods. Perhaps he never drew on that credit you gave him at all. Perhaps he just quoted you as a reference, when ordering, to show that he was good for a hundred pounds. That was the way he got his stock. But now he probably owes three hundred or four hundred or five hundred in various places, but his bank account is healthy."

The bank manager was suddenly serious.

"We can't look after the wholesalers," he said. "They have to watch themselves. They've met that trick before."

"It would be interesting to you, though," the sergeant said, "if Clemens now had a large sum, say five hundred in his bank account, and he drew it all out in cash one day."

"And to you?" the bank manager said pensively. "You have reason to think that that might happen?"

"No, Richard," the sergeant said. "We must be careful. I'm not warning you against this man. I won't say I don't know something of his past, because I do. But all that would interest me would be if he had more than that in his bank account. Some unexplained figure. Say one thousand or two thousand or ten thousand pounds. That is the kind of figure that would worry me, while you would be right to be worried if it was five hundred."

The manager got up. He left his desk and went through a door while the sergeant remained sitting in the chair. It would have been possible, the sergeant knew, for the manager to call someone else to do the work he wished to do. But the length of the manager's absence was conducive to the thought that he was consulting the books himself.

When he came back he bore no paper. His expression revealed nothing. He closed the door and crossed to his desk and sat down there. After a hesitation, he said:

"I shouldn't tell you this. Yesterday he had a credit balance of five hundred pounds."

"You mean he drew it out?" the sergeant's tone was quick. He was thinking of Harper and the pressure that must have been exerted on Clemens, and the temptation to cut and run.

"He paid it out," the manager said. "He paid his creditors, the five that he quoted us as a reference to in the first place. I don't know how his accounts stand with them. But from the small amount of credit they would give him from what we told them, I would guess he's in the clear."

They sat there marvelling at a man who, dealing in small sums, in figures which no real businessman would think of as more than the small change on the end of an account, had yet achieved that kind of balance that businessmen as a whole so rarely did.

"Of course," the manager said, "this may be merely round one. A balance at this stage, prompt payment, may be just the sprat to catch the mackerel."

"I shouldn't think so," the sergeant said. "I really wouldn't think so."

"Yet you say he has a past?"

"Not that kind of past."

"What kind of past?"

"A past that made me wonder about him. A present, too. But not one to make me prejudge him. I'd recommend that thought to you. You'll be cautious of him naturally, because he is a stranger. Me too. And yet so far as I'm concerned, you said it. He's in the clear."

In the clear, the sergeant thought, walking home. In two ways. Or if not in the clear, at least to be tolerated. For it was not only that Clemens had not cut and run, but had remained to face it out despite whatever threats Harper had made, knowing that suspicion would be sown in the minds of the police and that that suspicion might reach even the manager of his bank. It was the greater thing, the subtler thing, that was present in the sergeant's mind.

Clemens had not squealed on Harper. He had not reported an attempt at blackmail. Despite his visit to the police station, he had not expected the sergeant to fight his battles for him. Why?

# CHAPTER NINE

$S$O this, Clem thought, was it, and now it was beginning. He stood lounging at the corner, and no
thought of Harper or The Squirrel or other under-
world connections even crossed his mind. He looked
intently at the school. Through the screen of trees and
bushes, he watched a particular portion of the door.

He had forgotten Harper even as he had antici-
pated him. It had been weeks ago and he had dealt
with him as efficiently as he had dealt with the sergeant and the bank manager, as deliberately and with
as much preknowledge as he had settled himself in the
town of Eventham. But not quite was the sergeant
dealt with. The sergeant was involved in this too.
He thought of him, of his certain knowledge that he
was on duty at the station that afternoon, as he first
looked casually at his watch and then, with a particular intensity in his gaze, saw a tiny quiver of the fanlight above the door that he was watching.

An inner door had opened, into the hall behind
that fanlight. He had a sense as though he had
dwelled in them of the physical shapes, the nature
and geography of those old brick houses, mellowed or
ivy-clad, each withdrawn behind its garden's leafy
screen, in that long row, that special district of the
town. He had been there long enough, he had looked
long enough, he had investigated, followed, and in-
ferred, until he had an all but perfect sense of time

and place in Eventham. He would not have been there, would have known it to be useless to be there, had it not been a certain hour of a Wednesday afternoon, the early closing day, and the time, he had established when both he was free, and another, so that they both, by chance, if he had allowed the slightest shade of chance to enter, might have met while walking in the streets of the uncrowded, shuttered town.

He imagined her doing what she had to do. He guessed it was putting on a hat and coat, the particular hat and coat for whatever her purpose was at that hour of a Wednesday afternoon.

He was not concerned with her purpose. Whatever it was, after three months now, after a whole month now since the Harper episode and his establishment of himself as having credit at the bank, his solidification as it were of his union with the town, he did not propose that she should accomplish what she set out to do that afternoon.

He could see the top of the door above the hedge, and he saw it open. He quietly stood upright and prepared to move. In the resulting vacancy of where the door had been, he saw a movement. As soon as he saw the hat appear, saw it move forward, turning, as the door swung to, and then saw it disappear again as she descended the steps and started down the drive, he walked off, quietly, unhurriedly, down the avenue away from her and round the block.

Unhastening, he followed a course that a month's observation had told him was the right one. He moved towards the centre of the town, towards the streets where there were no gardens, and where, though the shops were closed, there were still people, pedestrians at leisure, and people in doorways, to a chosen scene.

It was a long straight road where he would see her coming in advance. He surveyed it carefully, having chosen beforehand the precise spot to within a hundred yards. He saw, with the certainty of fate, the location that fate had ordained to him. There was a man, near the open door of a house that fronted on the pavement, who was washing his car at the pavement's fringe. Across the road of the humdrum, towny street, other doors were open and people at them. Pedestrians were at hand but not too many.

He put his back to the street and looked into the window of a closed shop. If it had been open he would have entered it and bought some item. Since it was closed he could look as though he had hoped to enter it. He could see her coming, far down the street. In the reflection of the window he could see a woman at a door across the street who was talking to a child.

She was now as far on the other side of the car as he was on his. He turned from his window and began to walk towards her. The man washing the car was on his knees on the pavement doing something to a wheel.

Clem had the chance to see her whole and in her entirety, to see, as a stranger might, the effect she made on the world at large. He wondered why the "sensible" shoes. Would not a woman in her position make a better impression with taller heels? Or were the shoes some response to some image she had once had of herself as an outdoor girl? The coat was surely a demonstration of the unfulfilled widowhood of the natural spinster: the longing, if not real at least apparent, not for experience in the present but in the past. The hat was indescribable. If the best *chapelier* in Eventham had set himself with all the art at his disposal to imitate the least inspired product of the worst, to produce the least striking credible female ornament, as a satire on the taste of English women, that might have been the product, infinitely expensive no doubt, which he would produce.

Clem could see her and examine her every detail because they were only twelve yards apart. They were going to pass immediately opposite the car owner with his bucket. Clem altered course slightly, not passing, but straight towards her.

It seemed, for an instant, that she could only see his feet. As he moved one way, so did she. When he dodged again, she moved once more, and still, not until they were actually in that state of indecision of two pedestrians meeting, each over anxious to give way to the other, did she look up and see his face.

He stopped, straight in front of her, in a moment of deliberate confrontation.

He had not known what she would do then. It did not matter what she did. His plans were laid. In fact, she looked quickly at him, with that uncertain elusive glance that she must bestow on every man. She was actually beginning to look away when she looked again.

She went white. She had halted in mid-stride, with an "Excuse me" on her lips. He was not prepared for the instantaneous nature of her reaction. Her knees slowly buckled. She fainted on the pavement.

"Christ!" said the man with the bucket.

Clem was with her instantly. He stood over her. He did not touch her. His attitude, his whole expression, was one of bachelor helplessness.

"She seemed to stagger," he said defensively and excitedly. "Who is she? Do you know her?" His reaction time had been deliberately slow. He had not been prepared for a complete collapse. But he was in the part now, had committed himself, temporarily as it must be. He watched her closely for any sign of coming round.

"Hell, Mate!" the bucket clattered. "Can't you lift her head up?"

The man was already on his knees beside her, giving her the same tender solicitude he had bestowed upon the car.

"We'd better find out who she is," Clem blandly said. "And get her home."

There were footsteps: the woman from across the street and others from all along the road.

"Give us a hand," the man said. "We'll get her in the car."

It was the reality of the scene, the fact of it, his inability to understand that such could result from his contrivance, which mildly impressed itself on Clem. It left him lost, with a whole world of un-understanding somewhere. He found himself actually handling her legs, a situation that went beyond his dreams, as she stirred and gasped and they lifted her into the car.

"It's Miss Smith!" a woman said excitedly. "The mistress from the private school!"

"Look, friend," Clem said, quietly backing away. "I'm going to leave her to you."

No one heard him. There were too many people now, talking all at once, the women saying that they should not have touched her, should have left her stretched out on the pavement. And he did not want to be heard. The touch of her, the slide of silk on flesh, had somehow badly affected him. He backed away to the corner, conscious that one woman at least had turned and looked at him indignantly, as though suspecting he had struck the victim. But on reaching the corner, he turned and went.

He went quickly. It was the most crucial time of all. Either he would succeed or his whole carefully erected edifice would collapse about his ears. He crossed the town for a distance of a quarter of a mile. He came to the police station.

He had no need to pretend, as he had thought he would have to do, to be excited and distressed. When the constable saw him, and heard the first of his story across the counter, he gave him the slow look of a man in a state of caution verging on alarm.

"The sergeant," Clem said insistently. "I have to see the sergeant. He knows what I'm talking about, and you don't."

The sergeant looked puzzled when he appeared. He had thought he had heard the last of Clem, at least from Clem.

"Does she live here?" Clem demanded rather than asked of him. It would be wrong to say he played his part. It was playing him. "Emma Smith—is she a resident in this town, or what connections has she got here?"

"Look," the sergeant said quietly. "You just tell me. What have you been up to?"

The little room with the counter across the middle, darker and dimmer in daylight than when the light was lit, had its own routine in crises. When it happened, the sergeant and the constable stood firmly there and looked at it.

It was a strange kind of crisis they were dealing with.

Clem looked slightly dazed. Clem was slightly dazed. He was hardly clear enough to get away with it. That he should actually be acting so artificially true a part left him himself surprised. They could not believe him, he thought. It was quite impossible. And yet they must. They knew, in detail, every item of his coming to the town.

"I met her," he said, standing up before the counter. "This woman, Emma Smith. The one who accused me at my trial. The one who sent me up for five years! She's here!"

"Who?" the sergeant said. "Who are you talking about?"

The constable said: "Emma Smith."

"Sergeant!" Clem said, with all the outraged indignation of despair. "You know when and why I came here. But did you know that she was here? For God's sake why didn't you tell me if you did?"

They got it out of him slowly, or they were getting it out of him slowly, when there was a squeal of car brakes outside the station.

He did not dare to look. He knew who it would be. He had been only just in time.

Emma Smith entered, supported by the man who had the car on one side and by the woman from across the street on the other. They looked helpless and afraid. She looked mad. It was her pallor and the dishevelment of her dress.

"That's him!" she said hysterically when she saw Clem. "They've arrested him already!"

"The lady," the man who supported her told the constable, "wants to make a statement to the police."

"She's from the girls' school," the constable whispered to the sergeant.

The sergeant turned to Clem. He lifted the flap of the counter:

"You'd better come through here."

Clem knew the type of small room he was taken to and left in. He had been in one before. It was not quite a cell. That came later.

He could hear the voices talking endlessly on outside. First it was Emma Smith, and then the man who had brought her in his car, and then the woman from across the street. He could not tell what they said, and the sergeant's replies were quite inaudible. They went on and on, and even then they did not end but simply died away.

There was left the subdued muttering of the constable and the sergeant talking.

It was half an hour before the door opened and the sergeant came in. He was frowning, as a man does when he is contemplating something approaching the necessity for disbelief. He said nothing as he joined Clem, the two of them standing in the little, sparsely-furnished room.

"She was the one?" he said at last. "She was the one who identified you and sent you up on a seven-year sentence?"

"I've got to get out of this town," Clem said bitterly. "If she lives here, I've got to go. I don't see how I can. It's going to break me, having to sell the business."

They contemplated one another with a mutual, hopeless outrage.

"The man with the car," the sergeant said, "the man who brought her here, though he thought she ought to go to the hospital—he said you simply met in the street in front of him. Her story is different. You didn't molest her, did you?"

Clem said: "Oh, God! Suppose I'd met her in the night and near no one with a car!"

The sergeant was examining him slowly, looking for the least sign of some reason or intention behind circumstances that must have been to him incredible.

"You'd be wiser," the sergeant said, "not to let that happen."

"But if I stay here!" Clem said. "If I don't leave the town at once—"

The sergeant waited, wanting to hear the end of that sentence, which did not come. They were left, the two of them, considering Clem's position in a town where sooner or later he was sure to be accused of annoying an innocent female citizen, or even, if the alleged situation warranted it, of actual rape.

The sergeant had put his hand in his trousers pocket. He had found some change there. He jingled it.

"What happened the first time?" he inquired. "The time you were sent to gaol for? Was it like this afternoon?"

Clem looked at him almost stupidly. The man was a sergeant of police and he was asking him, after a seven-year sentence, five years actually served, whether he had been innocent of the crime or not.

"What's the use of my telling you," he asked bitterly, "that I never even saw her?"

The sergeant went on jingling his change. Or perhaps it was a key ring.

"I wouldn't say it wouldn't be a good idea for you to leave the town if you got the chance," he said.

Clem turned away from him. He looked at the obscured windows that cast a ghastly light.

"I was lucky with that shop," he said theatrically. "I was lucky with Eventham altogether."

"Don't rush it," the sergeant said. "Don't lose too much sleep over it either, now we know her type."

His voice was flat. He was willing to wait. Perhaps, after all these years, he was interested in a case. He was willing to wait and see.

Clem wondered. He was left in a state of mild amazement. He had got it over, the initial meeting. The sergeant had apparently accepted it: that after three months living in the town he had found the woman there, the one woman, the important one, the one he should escape, by meeting her in the open street. And her reaction had been true to type. She had gone so far as to carry the sergeant with him.

It was a most fortunate beginning. But also it was only a beginning. It was the next step, the step the sergeant did not even dream of yet, that would call for the utmost caution.

# CHAPTER TEN

THE sergeant called on Miss Emma Smith a week later. He gave her the week to recover, allowing her that period for her own mind to deal with her meeting with the man, to acknowledge, if possible, that she had met him, that he was there, living in her town, and that nothing had happened.

The sergeant went in plain clothes and not as a part of duty. It was not the sergeant's duty to investigate crimes long since dead and of which both trial and sentence had long since been carried out. If there was duty at all involved it was no more than to investigate allegations that had been made in his hearing in the police station, and of those it could not be the facts which could be investigated, since they had already been disproved, but only the cause. And to investigate causes could not be said to be part of a sergeant's duty.

He walked across the town. It was again a Wednesday afternoon, though not this time a Wednesday when he was on afternoon duty at the station. It was with the unhaste of leisure that he entered the school grounds, pausing for a moment in the shadow of the trees and hedges and looking at Victorian building: at the expanse of brown brick and the black of the windows which, by some trick of light or the shade of the trees across them, had acquired a complete opacity.

A young woman came round the building, short-skirted, tweedy. Behind her walked a crocodile of girls in hockey clothes. They were heading for the gate and he saw the secret of the Wednesday afternoon, that it was the sports day. In the face of the dawning outrage of the young sports mistress that he, a man, should be lurking in the grounds, he went to the door and rang the bell. The crocodile moved past and away from him with backward glances, and the building seemed to radiate the silence of an emptiness.

Too late? It was only two o'clock and neither the mistress nor the girls had told him there was no one in.

The door opened. It was a tall thin girl in gym slip and blouse who opened it into the vernal hall, and her attitude, when she saw him and he told her he wished to see Miss Emma Smith, was that of one who did not know if she had done right to do so. "Will you please wait here?" she said, and pointed to a precise spot on the polished floor just far enough inside the hall for her to close the door behind him.

The hall was darker when the door was closed. Illuminated only by the fanlight it had a silence as of a church. The girl tiptoed to a nearby door and knocked on it. The sergeant heard no reply while she waited, listening intently, but she went in.

Perhaps she thought he was a parent, he speculated, as indeed he was, though his children did not go to this school. She could place him perhaps, even the girl, as the type of parent to whom sending a child to this school would be an effort and an essay into fields that were quite unknown. Parents, he thought, arriving at the school, should do so in cars: in pale blue, bulging, glittering cars for the social women and black long-lined limousines for the men. If he were a parent, and were visiting the school, he would have to be segregated and kept at a distance from his children.

She came back, the girl, and said almost soundlessly: "Will you come this way?" She held the study door open but only half open so that not until he reached it and rounded it could he see what lay inside.

A facade, he thought, of pathos. He looked at the desk, the book-case, even before he looked at Miss Smith sitting diminished by the furniture that she must at some time have so bravely bought. And yet she was successful. The school worked. She had attracted pupils to it. Perhaps the secret was her very air of faded gentility, of diminished grandeur, and the non-religious, non-modern, un-everything, and even un-colourful pictures on the walls.

"Mr. Huntley?" she said, looking up with an academic appearance from her desk.

It was impossible, the sergeant thought, to correlate the appearance of her as she sat there, in control with the effortlessness of pure gentility, with the other appearance she had had, at the police station, of being a half-mad woman.

She said: "I don't think we've met before. Will you take a seat?"

The sergeant looked cautiously behind him as he did so. The door was closed; the girl had disappeared. "Sergeant Huntley," he said. "We met at the police station a week ago."

She had been holding a pen. She had been fulfilling some busy academic image in her own mind. Now she was rigid. He was not quite sure of the initial pallor, but he detected, after a moment, the faintest flush.

"I understood from you that that incident was closed," she said.

Just that. She evidenced no surprise at the transformation of her guest from a prospective parent to a sergeant of police. Perhaps it was automatic in her mind, the possibility that people were not what they seemed. And she was even coolly resentful, putting him in the wrong. Had he not disbelieved her on the occasion to which she referred? The fact that he had believed the bystanders, those who had seen what happened, and not she, who had fainted, would always be held against him.

"Not closed," he lied. "As I told you then, Miss Smith, it was merely that we could not possibly make a case against him."

In fact, he wondered if her egotism was complete. Or perhaps, he thought, her mind was just a closed system, infallible in the room, her study, infallible in all its contacts with mistresses who were her employees, infallible in its dealings with girls whose very purpose was to be there to receive instruction. He wondered at the extent to which she was dependent on her own authority, on the fortunate chance that had given it to her and so perhaps prevented a possible breakdown.

She took off the glasses she was wearing, the glasses that seemed more part of the appurtenances of her study, a property like the desk, the book-case, rather than an aid for eyes.

"Just why have you come to see me, Sergeant?"

He said : "Has he troubled you again, the man?"

She was holding the glasses on the desk before her, and she looked at them.

"I gather," she said, "from the evidence and the

stories that were told to you in the police station, that he could not have been said to trouble me in the first place."

The sergeant was alert at her evasion. He wondered why she troubled to evade. She had no need to do so.

"I was referring to the time when I understand he really did trouble you," he said. "Five years ago. Don't misunderstand me, Miss Smith. You seem to be taking the attitude that I called you a liar the other day. It isn't that at all. I can quite well understand the shock of meeting the man again, quite suddenly, in the town. That there should be some confusion about what happened is completely natural."

He saw the glasses bend. He would not have been surprised if they had snapped. She was affected by his explanation, unduly affected by it. Perhaps she regarded it as a kindness or a lifeline.

"It isn't easy for me to talk to you about this, Sergeant," she said after a moment's pause. "I don't want to become again involved in a wrangle about whether he did or did not make an overt gesture."

The sergeant said simply, with all the directness that was his character: "Have you seen him since?"

She looked up from her glasses. She stared straight at him with eyes behind which he could see nothing, as though either he or she were looking through a mist.

"It seems to me, Sergeant, that if I am not to be believed on my unsupported word, it would be better for me not to discuss the matter."

The sergeant was stopped. He was led to an incredible thought. Was he investigating the past or the present of the case, he wondered? But there could be no present. If he had been sure of anything, on entering, it was that.

"Miss Smith, if he has been worrying you, you must surely tell us. One meeting, mere chance, was nothing. But a second meeting within a week—if there happened to be a third, then there would be a case. Annoyance is something we can really deal with."

He spoke sharply, more sharply than he had intended. For he would not, could not, let her get away with it. To allow her insinuations that she did not have to substantiate would make the situation worse than if he had never come at all. And he was utterly sure that there had been no annoyance. The man Clemens would have had to be mad not to cross the street away from her on any occasion that he saw her in the distance.

"No, Sergeant," she said with a female precision which was itself an insinuation, "he has not been annoying me."

The sergeant took time to think. The interview was not going in the direction he had intended. To ask whether Clemens had troubled her again had been no more than an opening gambit. Following that, he had intended to ask her to tell him again in detail her version—perhaps a new version—of what had happened the previous week. From that he would have been able to lead on, insensibly, to what had happened five years ago. The two stories, the sergeant thought, would throw some light on one another, even if the conclusions he came to had to be kept entirely in his own mind or stored against some future time when Miss Smith might make some accusation against someone else.

The sergeant was experienced. He had known the relevance of his undertaking of that afternoon to the future. He was no psychologist. It was from a practical point of view that he pondered over the developing character of a woman.

"Good," he said, with all the stolidity of his position in her chair before her desk. "You haven't seen him again then?" He gave every indication of wanting to go on from there.

Her gaze had withdrawn. She was looking at her glasses, sadly, as though speculating on the torture to which her fingers sometimes put them. The sergeant himself had begun to wonder why he was insisting, driven by her obscurity to insist on her negation of something he oddly feared as much as he regarded it as incredible.

"I said," he said, almost brutally, very much the male now in the female sanctuary, "that you haven't seen him?"

"I did not say that," she said.

Her phrase seemed to lie, like her glasses and her glasses case, on the white blotting paper on the desk between them.

Mentally, the sergeant groaned. He cursed himself for his inability to leave well alone. He wondered if the fact that he was not on duty would offer him the excuse to take no official cognisance of what she said.

He waited for her to tell him, and she did not. It was then that he reversed his attitude, treating her at last, as he had intended to do in the first place, as someone who must be humoured.

"You might tell me," he said gently, "when and where."

She lifted up her eyes to him and returned his gaze. "Is it any business of yours now?" she said.

He wondered. The astonishing fact was that she was convincing him. For the first time, after all her obscurities and evasions, it came to him that she might be, must be, referring to some kind of truth: not that that prevented him even for a moment from ceasing to regard it as quite incredible.

"I am, Ma'am," he said, giving a gentle inflection to the formal words, "involved in your protection."

She regarded him coolly and quite distantly. "It is a type of protection on which I no longer feel I can rely."

The sergeant realised he had been a fool. He had equated hallucination with some kind of mental deficiency. It always had been in his experience prior to that case. Now he realised that it could be, was, associated with the other thing. He had been outwitted, and he had no truth left to hold his hand on.

His attitude took on, at last, humility.

"Miss Smith, you've told me something that leaves me at a loss."

"But you have no right to inquire," she said. "Least of all to interfere. I have not complained to you. In fact, I would no longer think of that as the wise thing. Would it be saying too much to say that you—not you personally, but the law—has failed?"

Bewildered, completely bewildered now, he said: "You mean you've seen him and you want to see him?"

"You didn't reform him, did you?" she said. "In the five years you had him, you did not reform him in the slightest."

The sergeant sat there looking appalled, as indeed appalled he was, by her saintly tone.

He waited for her to say more, but she did not. Twice he opened his mouth, only to realise that he was doing what she had just told him he had no right to do: inquiring. But as for a statement, what could he say? Caution her as though she were a girl, she whose imagination had always shown itself more than alive to the risks she ran? Or say simply that he did not believe her, that she was imagining this as she had the rest?

He reached suddenly for the corner of her desk, where he had laid his hat.

"If I have any complaints to make, Sergeant," she said, smiling distantly, "I'll come to see you."

He got up. Helplessly, fish-like, he said: "Yes, you do that." He blundered towards the door.

She did not let him out. The girl was waiting there, to show him through the door. Even that shocked him, that Miss Smith must have known the girl was in the hall and had not taken steps to see that she was removed from any chance of listening. But then, perhaps to Miss Smith their whole conversation could have been shouted in a public square.

He went back to the station. Sergeant Pearley was on duty.

"What's eating you, Huntley?" Pearley said as he came in.

"I'm damned if I know," he said, looking at his opposite number with a kind of outrage. "I don't know if I've been investigating the more stupid irrelevances of a woman's mind or the beginnings of a murder that hasn't happened yet. Or perhaps the middle. It would explain it. The feeling of entering in the middle of the picture."

"You want to go round with the Social Worker,"

Sergeant Pearley said with sympathy only for himself. "There are six would-be murderers on Commercial Row alone, and in most of them the beneficial victims would be children."

# CHAPTER ELEVEN

THE room behind the shop grew stifling towards ten o'clock at night. It was a small room, like all the kitchen rooms behind the rows of houses, but he had put a large bulb in the electric light socket. The result was to show up every mark on the wallpaper and every bruise on the cheap second-hand furniture which he had dared to buy. The passage of time was a strange combination of glare and silence, an emphasised aloneness of barren minutes succeeding one another.

At a quarter to ten, he watched the clock. At ten o'clock he went to an alcove and took out a dark coat and hat. He put them on. Then he switched the light out and stood there in the darkness. It was after his eyes were accustomed to the darkness that he opened the back door quietly and moved out into the small back yard. He stood there listening and it was moments before he soundlessly opened the outer door of the yard and stood there, too, for a moment, looking to right and left along the backs, his body still in the heavy shadow. He stepped out and closed the door behind him, and walked quickly to the junction of the side road.

He was free then, with the sense of freedom of anonymity. He went through the town, hesitating at each corner as he came to it, looking down each road before he passed down it. Seeing a policeman down one road, and a car with lights on down another, he avoided both. He walked down a third, where he was the only pedestrian passing from one street lamp circle to the next between the rows of houses with lights in their bedroom windows. And all the time the sense of freedom, of the unfettered ability to do anything, was increasing in him.

His breath came more quickly as he entered the vicinity of the school. It might be at any time now. He inspected the roads more carefully as he came to them. They were empty, and he passed the school itself. But he knew which way to go. He knew her direction and the way she travelled, down past the park and towards the river.

He knew the way she must go, not because he had followed her, though that he had done, but because she was herself. Just as, five years ago, in that other town, she had found herself in the one part of the suburb where she would be alone, and shadowed by the trees, so now she must, not might but must, go down to where the park sloped downwards to the river, and a path, a narrow road ran between the bridges, lonely and only half illuminated, though at no great distance from her school.

His expectation increased as he walked down the avenue beside the park. Since someone, exercising a dog, was coming up, he crossed the road. At the bottom, he stood for a moment on the bridge itself, even in the circle of the street lamp, looking down on the night-glistening water. Then he moved, as though suddenly disappearing, along the narrow path.

He was walking close to the bushes, in the shadow, away from the grass-fringed river bank, when he saw her. And he stopped. Thin and prim in a pale mackintosh, with a hood of the same material enclosing her head, she stood beneath a street lamp, namelessly trysting, with a symbolism, a nakedness of intention, which even she must surely understand.

He had been silent in his approach to her, and yet she was aware of him. She was turned in his direction, watching, patient, neither retreating nor inviting. He let her wait and watch and yet she still remained, with the same passivity, watching the position where, though she could not see him, she must know that he was.

He moved forward gently, stalking her, though she must know his every movement. He stopped within ten yards of her, too aware of the danger of a sudden approach or rush.

"Emma," he said quietly. "Emma Smith."

He could see her face now, half shadowed by the hood but pale and expectant in the lamplight.

He moved one pace forward, speaking her name again, inviting her to come to him, though he knew she would not, but saying it all the same, almost silently in the night, as a man might call some half-wild creature's name. There was a mist upon the river, and forming a halo beyond the lamp light, so that the evening, the night itself, was similar to that occasion so long ago when they had failed to meet.

She stood where she was. She spoke primly, in a schoolteacher's accent, with clear diction though in a tiny voice:

"Your friend the sergeant came to see me this afternoon."

He stopped. He looked quickly around him at the bushes. The movement was instinctive, born of a sudden fear. And then the feeling rushed back into him.

No, she would not do that. He was more sure of her than of the movements and actions of any other person. She would not destroy the situation while there was any prospect of its continuance.

"He wished to know if I had been troubling you again?" he asked her mockingly but almost silently, his eyes and ears alert for sound or sight of anyone approaching from either side.

"He asked me if I had seen you again," she said interestedly. She was still standing where she had been. From the beginning to the end of his approach to her, now that he was within five yards of her, and they were enshrouded almost intimately in the night, she had not moved.

He waited. Her words were such as to give him pause, perhaps to make him retreat again by the way he had come, as she must know. There was an innocence about her figure beneath the light that was belied in fact. It was not her lack of faith he feared, but her ingenuity, the very opposite of innocence, which must exist somewhere in her mind.

"I could not deny it," she said in the same interested tone, spacing her remarks to the shadow, which must be all she could see of him. The impression was strong that she was putting him through some form of terror, an incipient threat in which he himself was expected to half believe.

"So?" he said sardonically. "You told him where and when?"

"Harold!" she said, and in another moment she was in his arms, half way between the light and the position where he had been.

They kissed. Her eyes were closed. Her lips were no longer prim now, no longer those of the school mistress, but avid, drawing their energy and their imagination perhaps from the remembered images of cinema screens. Her body quivered. Lightly clothed beneath the mackintosh it was shivering even before he touched it, from the cold.

All the time they kissed, his eyes were open, watching not her but the path to right and left. His trust was limited to the situation only in which they were alone. It was the possibility of the approach of another person that inspired the fear in him.

"Some night," he said flatly, when her head drew back though her arms still held him, "Some night it will not take me so long to reach you. Instead it will be you who will come to me."

Her answer was to press her body to him with a motion as piteous as it was appealing.

He broke from her, turned and took her arm. They began to walk slowly along the path, leaving the circle of light and moving into the darkness towards where the next light shone dimly in the distance.

"Have you thought any more," he said calmly, "about me and you?"

She broke into a hurried, excited, lover's speech, and he did no more than listen to her as they walked.

"It was such a pity," she said. "So much of our lives were wasted because you did not approach me carefully, as you did tonight, that other time, five years ago. If I could only have taught you then what you could have had instead of that brutal taking! But now you are an ex-convict, and I, in my position—believe me, Harold, I have thought!"

In the darkness, and sure that there was no one near them, he essayed something he had not dared before.

"You're sure it was me?" he said. "Whoever it was attacked you that other time?"

"Why!" she said, with a world of reproach in her tone. "Of course it was you; there was no one else!" To her, the latter part of her statement implied the former. "Oh, Harold," she said distressed. "That's another thing. If only I could teach you not to lie!"

Seeing nothing in the darkness before them, he contemplated the situation as it was, looking back perhaps on the means whereby he had brought it within his control.

"You may succeed in doing that," he said, merely speaking the words, putting them out as though to try them, to see what effect they had.

"Oh!" she breathed, like a girl, like a young girl bride who believes she can reform her husband. "If I only could!"

He paused in his walking. It took his utmost endeavour, his maximum capacity of control, not to stop or stumble. She was aware of his hesitation, must be, and yet her mind, her preoccupation with her own thoughts, prevented her from registering it. By exercising his control he was able to continue with her as they were, resuming again, as though nothing had happened, without her looking up to see what had.

In the circle of the light before them, nearer now, by the river's edge, so that even its base was a misty image, he had seen the passing of a policeman with his bicycle. A policeman pushing his bicycle, with its light out, coming straight towards them.

He had to think quickly. It was the one situation he had feared. He had to calculate the misty unknown of her mentality. For a fraction of an instant he thought of breaking from her, of running the other way. Yet he knew the result of that, the sudden break, the inexplicable action. In his imagination he could already hear her scream, as he had heard it once, five years previously, on such a misty night. And he could guess the consequences, the story she would tell.

"Listen," he said calmly, with superhuman restraint. "There is someone coming along the path towards us."

Her answer was to grip his arm the tighter and to move her body to him. Yes, he thought. That was her answer when there was no one there. But the chance of actual meeting, and a police constable at that, was more of a risk than he had ever dreamed to take.

"A policeman," he said.

She said "Oh," indifferently.

Yes, he thought, but what when the man was actually visible to her, and coming towards them, and then when he had passed and was going away again. Could she resist the opportunity to attract attention, to portray a drama? He wondered whether to leave her, to walk on the opposite side of the road to her, so that the first thing the constable would see would be the evidence of their peace. But in the misty night he believed he could divine her feeling to an extent she had never achieved herself.

He chose the greater risk. With his hand on her arm, he stopped her and drew her to him. With exquisite care not to alarm her, his arm went round her shoulders. He made as if to kiss her while she stood against him like a young girl, stiff and quiet.

He was just in time. The policeman's lamp was suddenly alight and it shone full upon them. Her stiffness became rigidity as they were bathed by the circle of illumination in the darkness. He held her firmly, afraid that she would cry out or break away. But her rigidity was only momentary. While the light was still upon them, and before it was suddenly withdrawn, she had already relaxed and moved her face towards his, to kiss him avidly.

"Goodnight," the policeman said, his form a dark shape against the glimmer of the water as his footsteps went stolidly past with all the English policeman's capacity for seeing everything and seeing nothing while on a night beat.

The danger was past, but Clem was left with a woman who was not merely relaxed but spent, clinging to and almost hanging from him.

"Oh," she said inexplicably, murmuring in his ear. "If only I'd known you cared."

# CHAPTER TWELVE

THE sergeant went to the school a second time, but now, as he walked up the drive towards the door, he fingered a note in his jacket pocket. He had no need to look at it, to read it again. It said: "Would the sergeant who called on me a few weeks ago please care to call on me again?" On the telephone pad at the station, from which the note had come, had been scrawled the information that the caller who had delivered the message had been Emma Smith. There was even the mention of a time.

It was not a school, the sergeant thought, surveying the frontage of the building which he had to himself on that occasion. It was a monument, a monument to that social cupidity which was the property, in all the world, of the English middle class. Somewhere, from an upper room, he could hear a choir of girls' voices singing. The tune was a half remembered melody, pallid with time. Would they have learned a different tune if they had gone to the council school? He had to admit they probably would. There would have been more energy and less finesse in the singing, an energy derived, perhaps, from the fact that there would have been boys of those girls' own ages, perhaps eleven and twelve, to pull their hair, to indulge in talk and conflicts, or worse, which would have destroyed the illusion that the world was a romantic image. The girls of Emma Smith's school, he imagined, must grow up in a state of mutual fostering of that illusion in one another. '

Yet there were boys at the school. With the garden to himself the sergeant was unashamedly pausing in the drive, snooping as he would have called his interest in the building as a whole, though perhaps a reluctance to approach the front door, and to enter the closed atmosphere beyond it, had something to do with it. From a particular position near a bush by the middle of the short drive, he could see into a section of one of the ground floor classrooms. He could see three or four boys there, of ages six to nine, a portion of a single preparatory department class. Pre-sex, he thought. Or at least the pretence of pre-sex, as though there was an age below which boys were not boys but merely children, a theory which the sergeant, from the experience of his own family, regarded as dubious in the extreme. He pitied the boys for the ruder shock and awakening that would come to them when, so soon, they left the care of Emma Smith and went on to the boys' school, to mix with those who had unlearned their inhibitions.

One of the boys had seen him, was looking out of the window at him and nudging his nearest neighbour. The sergeant walked on and rang the door bell. As he stood waiting the singing above him ended and then began again, with a new and ragged tune.

He was surprised to see that it was Miss Smith herself who opened the door to him. She stood far back in the hall to allow him in and allowed him to close the door himself. It was as though there were established a conspiratorial intimacy between the two of them. Her very voice was muted, like the light when the door was closed, presumably lest they be heard in any of the nearby classrooms.

"I hope you didn't mind my saying between three and four o'clock, Sergeant. It's the time my class is taken with the others by the singing mistress." Having stood back to let him in, she now came forward again, past and round him, to precede him into her office.

He had minded. The duty sergeant who had taken the message had told him: "Your girl friend says three o'clock, and don't be late." The police, he had reflected, or at least that part of it of sergeant's rank and over, was not a public service of quite that order, not entirely employed for the exclusive convenience and protection of the class with property. But she was waiting for him, holding the inner handle of her office door.

"I presumed you had something to tell me," he said as he entered the room with its overpowering bookcase, its somehow feminine desk, and its pictures that were so unpositive as to be merely a convention, the kind of thing that a picture ought to be.

She stood by the desk and faced him, and that itself was unusual, he realised, creating as it did a hiatus, during which he too could not sit down but must stand and face her.

"It isn't so much to tell you," she said, "as to ask you." Then she blushed, quickly and wildly, looking at him hopefully, beseechingly, and, for an instant, abjectly. It was with the quick intention of covering her confusion that she hurriedly sat down, not because she would not have preferred to stand informally, at the end of the desk that was nearest to him. She moved papers on the desk with a vague intention, as though to clear a space for something that they were about to lay there, although there was no such thing.

It was coming back to him now, her equivocal attitude on the previous occasion. He sat with a deliberation the essence of which was caution.

"To ask me?" he said. He could not imagine what she had to ask him. So far as he was aware, what she had admitted on the last occasion was that she was seeing Clemens, deliberately and of her own volition. She had thus removed herself from the cognisance and the protection of the police. He had been aware that it could not stop at that, that there would be repercussions. But now his role seemed to be limited to the task of disillusioning her, to explaining the new conventions that governed the new situation that she had herself created.

But there was something subtly different, not only about the woman but about the room. He could not place it. Perhaps it was the vase of flowers on the window sill, though there was no reason, other than his lack of memory of them, why they should not have been there before. It was the pile of exercise books on a shelf behind her, too large a pile, as though the work was accumulating instead of being finished, always, in time to maintain the neatness and the order. For herself, there was, or had been, the startling blush, so causeless and so soon, and not so much an uncertainty as a new tentativeness of her manner. It added up to something, in the sergeant's mind, that he would rather not have been there to face.

She was looking at him pleadingly even then. She said: "It was a mistake of mine, something I did too quickly. I shouldn't have asked you here to see me."

He spoke with a deliberate obtuseness, the essence

of which was self-preservation. It was not that they did not understand one another, but that they did so too well.

"It's more usual for people to come to the station."

She did not appear to have heard him. She must have done so. No one with her training could possibly have failed to understand a phrase intended to put her at a distance. She must know that he was telling her to put her difficulties, if she had run into difficulties, which he was forced to conclude was the reason for his presence there, in the most formal manner possible. But she ignored him.

"It would be ridiculous to put you in the position of sponsor," she said, with a sudden brightly tentative air, offering him a gambit.

He sat stolidly in his chair, retreating constantly, becoming ever more, each moment, a sergeant of police.

"In loco parentis," she said, and laughed. "As though he were a child, which he isn't, or irresponsible, which he is."

He had to speak. It was not that he wished to get at the truth of what she was telling him, for he not only did not, but refused to speculate about it, fearing it, and adopting a mental attitude of complete negation. What he feared was that she would go on telling him, regardlessly, so that he would have it all without having had a chance to disassociate himself from what must be entirely her affair and something that she must think about alone, in that closed room.

"He?" he said. "Are we talking about Harold Clemens, the man we talked of last time?"

She looked startled. She said : "Who else?"

He was brutal, letting her get away with nothing

whatsoever. He said: "Has he been annoying you again?"

She sat on her own side of the desk looking at him neither shocked nor outraged but merely sadly, convicting him of a badness of taste that put him beyond her pale. He was made indignant even before she told him anything of what she had to say.

"It was that, wasn't it?" he said with the outrage of guilt. "It was that you complained of, Miss Smith, but then you began to see him of your own accord. You must see how that lets us out, so that we can take no action no matter what happens after that!"

And Clemens too, he thought. What game was he playing? A moth around a flame? He had had sympathy for Clemens, even believed he might have been wrongly convicted at one time. Now he could no longer regard him as quite so innocent, not even the apparent innocence of having turned up at the very town where his supposed victim had happened to arrive five years before he himself had the opportunity to do so.

"Sergeant," she said, lowering her eyes with an expression that he would have longed to call sanctimonious except that it was not, was rather honest to the very limits of what she, lacking self-knowledge, could think of as honesty: "There is something beyond mere justice. Some call it forgiveness, and some call it simply pity."

Which, he thought grimly, would make two of you. Each forgiving and each pitying. No, he thought, give me justice, even simple justice, rough and ready, and even wrong at times, so that when the innocents suffer they at least know they do so by mistake.

"So," he said heavily. "You were seeing him, Miss

Smith, last time I came here. Now you have forgiven him. But what is the next step, in that it could involve anyone of my profession? Is it simply that you have found cause to unforgive him again? Because if so, there isn't a court that would not say you have brought it on yourself. Unless—"

"Have I complained?" she said, looking at him now with a little hopeful smile.

It was the smile that told him. He had to fit it in with her tentativeness, with the pile of exercise books still uncorrected, the flowers: the fact that she also was what she had never been before. She was self-contained.

"Unless," he said, continuing stupidly in a line that he could even then see was outworn, "Unless, that is, he has been taking advantage of your good nature to take money from you."

She frowned her denial with a little expression of fear. He could see that he was wrong. She had given him no money. That indeed, the request for it, would have been the one thing to make her flee the greatest distance from him. And yet her reaction was positive. And he did not at first realise how excessive.

"Sergeant!" she said. Disconcertingly, tears had appeared in both her eyes.

She was wearing a dress of a black, silken, clinging material which emphasised the slope of her shoulders and fell about her arms, revealing their nakedness beneath its texture. Unbidden, as they looked at one another across the desk for what seemed an endless moment, a phrase came into his mind. It was as though, he thought, she had been bathed in grief: as though grief were some actual, clinging fluid and she had been dipped in it, so that now it dripped from her in some frozen, solidified texture. Yet her grief, her pain, was actual. It was that that he could not get beyond.

"Sergeant," she said slowly, helplessly, "What I asked you here to tell me was whether you could give me any further details about his record; whether I had anything else to forgive him for."

The peculiarity of her meaning was slow in coming to him. He was too immersed in himself, in his own nature and being, not to have an immediate reaction to what she said, a reaction dictated by who and what he was. It was overwhelmingly important to him that he should say what he had to say regardless, as though his own honour were at once in question, and nothing, neither her grief nor the significance of her meaning, could be adequate reason for with-holding his hand on that.

"If I knew of anything," he said, "I couldn't tell you. It isn't our business, as police, to hound a man. In a court, yes, we can reveal a criminal record. But not to chance inquiries. Not even in business, when one man may be taking a chance on another's faith. It isn't our business, Miss Smith, to perpetually destroy a man by bringing his past into the present."

He could not have said why he was so righteous about it, saying something that was not even completely true. Perhaps, he realised belatedly, that was why he did say it: because it was not completely true of all times and in all places. It was something he would have liked to be true, and which he would have liked to convince her was true, she who was still, to him, in some sense, a member of the general public or at least outside some inner and magic circle in which truth and wishful truth were somehow warped.

"It wasn't a chance enquiry," she said, quite helplessly now. "It was something I needed to know because of something that has arisen." Motionless behind her desk, she still had the air of wishing to demand what she had learned she must not, yet accepting, with the grief that seemed to be her natural role, the fact that she, her demand, were outside his notice.

Her meaning began to catch up with him then, her significant phrase "anything else to forgive him for". It did not prepare him as he sat before her, resentful and with-holding. It only sowed the ground with contingencies he had not imagined. He was in that state, even worse than if he had had no preparation at all, when she told him.

It was not exactly apology in her voice. Perhaps she had no idea that she had anything to apologise about. Since she had used that phrase it might even have seemed to her to be the opposite, that her act and attitude was one of magnanimity. Yet her restraint with him was certainly that justified by one who had shown his capacity clumsily to wound her.

"My question," she said, using words even then that might have related to an academic problem, "was because there is—might be—a possibility that I might marry him."

It was out.

The sergeant was still, stilled by a ghastly sense of his own inadequacy, by the defect of imagination, the plain, breath-taking unbelief even, that had caused him to lag so far behind her, so far under-rating her capacity that he had talked of business, as though that were the most important thing, while she, demure, sad, grief-stricken, so helpless and so easily wounded, had gone beyond any logical limit to a degree of acceptance unthinkable and therefore unimaginable to the male mind.

His own mind, indeed, turned and twisted. It took stock again of their situation in the room, of the flowers on the window sill, of her, the owner, principal and proprietor of the school, so endowed with power, dressed to the point of discretion and reserve, and yet so unskilled and innocent in the use of it. What could he believe: that in the clear cold light that flooded from the window into the room, he could see the naked woman beneath the dress? But that was no explanation either. That, at best, could explain *what*, but never *who*. It could explain *why*, but it never could explain the mental processes, the evasions, the deliberate innocences, the wilful or unwilful blindnesses that made to her, in that room, the why permissible. It could tell, he saw, the body, the female body beneath the dress, the uninteresting part of the story only. But the real story, the mental erection and superstructure that made that single phrase, and let her say it, even to him, a comparative stranger: that, he realised, was a thing of horror, of trembling unbelief.

"You," he said, openly incredulous now, with gaping disbelief, "marry him?"

If she had flushed, he could have understood it. If she had looked away, or burst into the tears that had already threatened, he would have found a grain of hope. But she answered his incredulity with all the self possession of the school mistress that she was: exactly as she might have answered the equal incredulity of some girl, telling her that she was to sustain some dire and over-adequate punishment for a misdemeanour, a heresy of conduct that the girl herself had not realised to be fatal until that moment. She answered, that is to say, entirely on the surface, escaping him as surely as if she had drawn a curtain across between them, at the very moment when he was at last prepared to understand the magnitude of what she had been freely telling him, forcing down the very throat of his unwillingness, until that moment.

"You are not permitted to make this public yet," she said. "No definite engagement has been announced."

If she had bludgeoned her truth into him with the strength that only mania could give to those frail arms beneath that dress, she could not have convinced him more thoroughly of her purpose. No mania indeed could have carried that conviction, a conviction born of tone, of the room, of the book-case and desk and the pile of uncorrected exercise books upon the shelf.

"So you will appreciate," she said distinctly, "my interest in and preoccupation with my fiancé's past."

For a moment, beneath the superficiality of her utterance, her forcing of him, her adoption of his own tone and far exceeding of it, the sergeant had a wild dream. He dreamed that he was in fact witnessing a kind of justice, the very happy-ending story that she thought it was: a man convicted for a woman's sake; forgiveness; reconciliation; the mutual dependence postulated in the beginning finding its acknowledgement at the end. He even tried to believe in it, as she must, faced with the sheer necessity of the facts. Yet in his heart, at the very instant, he knew it was impossible. It did not clear the air, their further conversation. Rather it took possession of them and led him up a peak of unreality he had never dreamed to scale.

"From him," he said with a precognition that at any other time would have been almost shrewd, "you will have heard—"

"Naturally, Sergeant," she said quickly. "You can't imagine that I doubt the word of a man I intend to marry. I am perfectly aware that he has committed no more than that one offence. But are you aware of it? Will the police even admit the possibility of the single offender? Or have you other suspicions, other charges waiting for him, if he should ever put a foot wrong?"

It was simply not in the sergeant's power to answer her other than directly. He might wish he had more to tell her. He might wish that he could return an answer that was at least equivocal. But he was not so much out of his depth as carried forward on a tide.

"There is nothing—" he said.

She was facing him directly, looking straight into his eyes.

"He himself will be glad to hear that," she said. "It was a reservation he made about our marriage, a fine reservation, since it indicated his regard and fear for me."

She got up. Now she had come directly to the point, the interview was at an end. The bewildered sergeant found himself preceding her to the door.

Why did he have, at that moment, a memory, a mental image, of Clemens' face? A pallor, he remembered, a peculiar wide-eyed earnestness that was far from the sardonic and yet which kept something, always, far behind the eyes. It was something to do with Clemens knowing, with his desire to know.

But he was in the hall again, accepting the formality of her restrained goodbye, then in the garden, in the open air, looking back at the closed door and the building, the very brick and stone, as though needing to convince himself that that was not insubstantial too.

She was deceiving herself about that, he thought. She could not surely imagine that her school, her way of life, would stand for it. Perhaps he did too. But yet she owned the property. Searching for Clemens' motives, he could only place that one: her possession of the property, and her money.

Or else, he thought, looking at the building, at the impressive permanence and value of it, and considering the shelter it gave, the security to at least one woman's life: or else, and more likely, Clemens had some other motive, something quite unspeakable.

## CHAPTER THIRTEEN

THE policeman's torch illuminated the two figures in the angle of the tree-dark corner of the suburban road. Two slim bodies, he saw, pressed close together. The man was a head taller than the woman, with his face turned down to her, caught pensively and oblivious in the sudden illumination of the night. The woman's face, upturned, with pursed lips; wore an equal oblivion, receptive and intent in what, until the light had disrupted their communion, had been a spaceless, secret, lonely dark. The policeman turned off his light. He had seen all he wished to see. The woman was no young girl in her early teens, determined on seduction while her anxious parents thought she was somewhere else. That kind, indeed, could no longer be expected to walk out from the town to where the suburb met the country and they found a precarious privacy in a leafy lane. The youngsters all had cars; and these, he had seen, were older: a married man perhaps stealing moments with his neighbour's wife. It was not his business. The policeman went his way, his footsteps receding round the farther corner of the road.

It was a pattern, Clem thought. It was she, she who now clung to him in willing subjection, and who had remained like that when the light had once again illuminated them, always a different light, and always in a different place: it was she who insisted that they met by night and loved clandestinely in the open, refusing with a half-truth, the statement that she could not be seen to go into his house with him so late at night, the actual privacy and comfort that his room afforded. Yet it was not that. He believed it was not that. It was no more that she in fact feared for her good name than that it was quite essential, as she said, that they should not meet in daytime, but only and always late at night, in darkness, walking across and round and away from the town until somewhere, each night, some chance would reveal them to a chance pedestrian, or, best of all, to the policeman on the beat.

She was relaxing now, and moving away from him just a little. Her movements were slow and satisfied, as after the passing of a crisis. She stood separately from him for a moment, collecting herself in the cool darkness, restoring her own identity, such as it was. She took his hand.

"It's time we went home now," he matter-of-factly said.

They began to walk, neither slowly nor quickly, for they had a long way to go. For a while she was silent, seeming to breathe the clean night air with that youthfulness, that unreal youthfulness, which had come to her, apparently, only when she was approaching middle age. She held his hand not as a girl might, but possessively, at times as though he were a child of hers.

"We must be practical," she said, echoing him, mocking him, "we have to think." She laughed almost silently, her body shaking, with a cynicism that momentarily revealed a true malevolence.

"We must try," he said steadily. "We can't go on like this. We have to plan."

Her laughter was completely silent now. It was through her hand that he could feel her body shaking in the darkness. He looked about him at the security of the houses, their reassuring solidity, their roofs against the sky, the occasional lights that were going out even in their bedrooms. He felt the impulse to touch the reassuring coolness of the hedges of their gardens as he walked. Every hedge wore shadows, and every garden was a clear and empty space beneath the sky.

"Come with me," she said insidiously, "into the school tonight."

"Emma," he said, still quietly, not putting undue force into his reproof. He was conscious of the distance, the depth of darkness, between one street lamp and the next.

"You're afraid," she said between her bursts of silent laughter. "You're afraid that I'll seduce you."

Indeed, he thought, with cold dark clarity, as innocent as the night, if she did not mean that, what did she mean?

"You don't mean it," he objected quietly. "Why talk like that?"

"I do!" She spoke suddenly, loudly, almost gaily, so that the words might have been heard suddenly through an open bedroom window, their irresponsible defiance spreading out in a wave across the empty gardens. "I do mean it! This time I do!"

He did not believe her, and yet he wondered. He wondered how far she had travelled, at least in times like that, in darkness, from not knowing what she thought to knowing finally what she wished.

He told her : "We must be careful."

But suddenly she began to speak, not loudly now but in an intimate whisper, not calling it out, so they could be heard, but in a thin, high ecstacy of release. She spoke continuously as they passed along the street, oblivious apparently of where they went. He imagined that she must know she was speaking, in quick, excited, partly muted words, clinging to him and pressing to him. Yet he wondered if what she was saying was passing the barrier of her knowledge : if she knew of it, or if, with the night as cover, it was escaping somewhere, at high pressure, from deep within her. Surely it could not meet with knowledge and pass through the gateway of the permitted, for it was not he but she who had established contact with some other level within herself.

He saw her face upturned to him, her moving lips, her eyes on him, regardless of the empty, silent street, of the pools of darkness that lay ahead.

"We can be alone, alone in my rooms," she said. "You can think. You can imagine. I won't speak. I won't say a word."

In the light of the street lamp, her cheeks had a greenish pallor. Her thin lips were almost black, jet moving lines at the outer edges where the lipstick still remained. But the fashion of her hurried secret speech was a sibilant breathing. He saw her little teeth and the damp tongue and the inner, paler edges of her lips. That what she said, offered, even pleaded to offer, was true, at least for the moment; that the mood might last right to, and through the actuality, he did not doubt. Her small eyes were staring, but it was not so much they as the lips that were prepared to swallow him.

"In my rooms," she said. "The girls. The girls' dormitary is next door. We will have to be completely silent. The girls are innocent, but they will be sleeping there, so near."

Peculiar, he thought: peculiar. She went on, virulent more than she was exciting, with an imagination that he did not know she had, and yet which he realised she must have had, though its expression had never seen the light of day nor even that of night. It had been there, he knew. He could not guess for how many years.

He listened. She talked as a lover might, excitedly, about future actual plans. He did not say a word, for he was not expected to say a word. Her need was to speak, and not to listen. He was left measuring the street length with his eyes, speculating: had he been aware that she was capable of this? He must have been, for now it had come he was not surprised. It was this, he imagined, for which he had suffered so long ago. But it was out now. It had risen to the point where he, if not she, could perhaps control it. Perhaps. He was conscious still of an uncertainty about the issue.

It was she again, talking as he listened to her. She harped upon the subject of the girls, their innocence, the extent to which they were in her charge. At first he failed to see the connection there, the extent to which her position in life, her responsibility, had charged her dream. Yet the proximity of her room to that of the girls was something she came back to, as though, in some sense, a violation of her would be a violation of them, of their innocence maybe, of their purity, that purity which must be itself a construction of her mind.

"We have boys, you know," she suddenly, insistently said. "Did you know we have boys at the school? We have to care for them."

He was highly conscious of the darkness, the emptiness, the loneliness of the street along which they walked. This, he thought, was a moment of danger for him. She began to indulge in what were, clearly, fantasies, about the boys. Her thoughts were ranging more widely, and with less and less restraint. It was his turn to imagine: to imagine her denouncing him, transferring the suggestions she was making from her to him. And credibly, he thought, for not only a court, but even the sergeant's ears, would disbelieve that she had thought of them herself. It was incumbent on him now to make a move, to break, to resist, and to cross the point of danger.

"Too soon," he quietly said. "Too risky. We won't until we're married."

It was not reproof. He had not dared reproof. He had not denied her images but transferred them to the future. But he said, echoing her cynicism, stirring, as it were, the dregs of her character:

"We'll sell the school. We don't want to destroy its value."

The other naked truth, he imagined, the mention of money, would restrain her as nothing else would. To her, he thought, in her present state, it would be the only other real thing, the other problem she had striven with all her life, pre-existent and perpetual. Ironically, it would feed her conception of the coldness, the masculinity as she saw it, of his character: the right reasons, the right apprehensions even, leading to the wrong conclusions.

He listened to his own voice speaking in the silent

night: dispassionate, unsurprised, and bearing no trace whatever of resentment, accepting even that what she had been saying had been the most natural thing in all the world.

Then when he finished:

"You think of everything," she said, pressing her body to him as they walked. Her face was still up-turned, the thin damp lips still parted, twisted now into a smile as of the Mona Lisa at last revealing her hatred of the bitterness of the world, her secret, so violent, never dared to be expressed before, at last divulged.

He was conscious of it then, what it was he had released, and was still releasing, through all these nightly meetings. Released, he thought with horror, and yet made normal. Warped and twisted as it was, it was still normal, still almost innocent girl-like sex, compared with what there must have been when it had been contained, compressed within her, inviolate, and too deep to be reached even by her own thoughts.

As they walked on, through the town now and to-wards the school, he thought with apprehension of the initial risks that he had run, when he had first dared to approach her after becoming aware of her noc-turnal habits. It filled him with fear now, the thought of that distant stalking, that revealing of himself at a distance from her along a road, waiting to see if she would faint again, as she had on seeing him in day-light. Not again, not ever in his life, would he ever have, for any task, such patience. He had played, he realised now, with lightning, with a thunder cloud that was super-charged, and this, this he was hearing now, was the charge leaking off into the ground.

"We were meant to be together," he calmly said,

keeping separate from her the compartments of his mind.

But what would succeed the charge, he wondered. He was aware, with an intelligence that belonged to the old Clem, that he was receiving suggestions—obscene suggestions impractical as they were pathetic in what she imagined to be their horror—as a psychiatrist might from a patient on his couch. But it was the succeeding normality he would have to deal with: the normality of a woman who had somehow ceased to live so long ago and who might, in the next stage begin to live again. It was that, he clearly saw, that he would be saddled with.

"That's the dormitory there," she said with the inner excitement in her whispering voice, for they had come into sight, distantly, of the school. "That's my bedroom window." For neither the darkness nor the distance were any barrier in the silence of the night in which they walked, for the imagination that was welling to the surface.

He wondered if he had contemplated, when he had begun on the course of action he had taken, its final consequence. If he had been a psychiatrist who could dismiss her. If he had been any normal man, any man not connected with her formerly in any way. But no normal man would have attempted what he had attempted. He would not have come near to her. That had been the trouble. Or he would have been afraid, shocked, and panic-stricken in the situation that was existent now. While for himself he was aware of his success, of his coming success, and also of the trap. Why was he not horrified, or panic-stricken, or afraid? Because he had seen that of the many outlets, there was one certain one?

It was his own mind that was veiled at that point.

"I must leave you here," he said, stopping firmly on the pavement beneath a tree while still fifty yards from the school.

"Come in!" she whispered excitedly, tugging gently on his hand.

He smiled in the darkness with the actual tenderness of knowledge.

"If I did," he said, "it would destroy everything between us and for ever."

She stood close to him silently, thin, dark, and fragile, looking down.

"We don't kiss in this street," he said. "We don't do anything more deliberately until we're married."

They stood silently together for a while, two shadows in the street, with no one there to see them.

# CHAPTER FOURTEEN

HIS motives, the sergeant thought; revenge or avarice.

He looked at the bridegroom.

The church was crowded. The youngest girls were at the front to see with their own eyes the beauty of an occasion the significance of which it could only be presumed they were not yet of an age to understand. In the second pews, and the third and fourth and fifth, were the classes in ascending order, all decked and beribboned in the school's vanity of its public show. At the back of the school, and at the end of each row beside the aisle, sat or stood the senior and the prefects, aware and conscious and adult and reverent as by their age they had every right to be, though no one had officially told them anything more than the youngest junior in the meantime. And behind the school there sat the parents, row upon row of smooth clean cloth and all the idiosyncracy of the women's hats. Even the few men present for their wives' and daughters' sakes, unwillingly in forced attendance to prevent the occasion being female altogether, or skulking on the back row, the sergeant saw, for purposes of their own, must have to admit, he quietly thought, that it was a happy and auspicious scene.

His gaze, having swept the church and rested on the back row, was arrested suddenly and momentarily.

There was Jackson there, the editor of the *Eventham Evening Chronicle*. It was easy to guess why he was at a social wedding. Beyond, he became suddenly conscious, the bride had appeared. Her staff, her ex-staff now, now that she had suddenly released them, and, as had been announced, had given up the school, were in attendance. Beyond, in pretty costumes, were the bridesmaids, the chosen girls.

Jackson turned and met his eyes. The sergeant stiffened. As Jackson turned again, to look at the bridegroom, the sergeant was suddenly aware that Jackson knew.

Of course, the sergeant thought surprised, he wants to know why I'm here. To avoid such uncomfortable implications he transferred his gaze right across the closed and ornamented and packed ranks in the crowded church to the position where the bridegroom stood.

He looked younger than she did, whether he was or not. He was a used object, the sergeant thought, under evident strain, got up to look respectable. And lonely. The best man was some other shopkeeper who had been pressed for the occasion, someone who, unlike Clemens, not merely owned but lived on his regular business, with no intention of selling it at a profit. Anyone, the sergeant thought, with half an eye, could see there was something wrong with Clemens. If he was buying businesses and working them up and selling them, as was rumoured, then he should have a businessman, not a shopkeeper, as his best man. And the church was full of the bride's connections, and he was there alone.

Money, the sergeant thought. The situation shrieked of money. He watched the service between the hats and heads and believed he saw, at one point, the bridegroom's lips twist in a naked grin of triumph. Or, he thought, revenge.

The respectable congregation sat stolidly through it all. A wedding was a wedding to them. The words meant what they said. When vice was enacted before their eyes they could not see it. The bridegroom and the bride were people, and because they put on a show, they forgave them. They even judged them by themselves, as the blind always did, believing that the motives of those who stood before the altar could be no different from those that would cause them to stand in that place. Or even less. In the very depth of their blindness they believed that no one else, certainly not these two, could have more thoughts, or more imagination, or a tenth the perversity that they had silently witnessed in themselves.

The sergeant was aware that Jackson was looking steadily at him all through the service. Already he had the foreknowledge that he was not going to be able to evade Jackson. He should spend time thinking of some explanation for his presence other than the actuality of a half-formed thought, a compulsion to witness something, for once in his lifetime, that was really strange and about which he had, or had had until Jackson appeared, exclusive knowledge. Instead he watched, putting Jackson out of his mind until the time came.

Both replies to the leading question were inaudible, the male one from self-consciousness, a sense of sin, and the female one from decorum, because it would have been impossible to shout it defiantly and triumphantly to all the crowded church: "I do; I will!" So thought the sergeant.

Jackson was standing but hanging back when the school began to file out, the small children from the front rows first, behind the bride's attendants. The sergeant had a momentary thought of pushing his way out early as though on urgent business. He knew he would have to go through with it. He made no move until the wedding breakfast party were all gone. Jackson, he guessed, must have turned up his files, and seen.

They met in the porch among the confetti and the remnants of the crowd, the comparative strangers who were watching the cars from the inadequate vantage of the steps. The constable was busy, fumbling with the traffic, harrassed by the pedestrians who stood around. The sergeant made no move to direct or help him. He filled his pipe, causing a deliberate obstruction on the steps, until Jackson was at his side.

"It's a long time," Jackson said grimly in his ear, "since I needed to buy information and co-operation from you with a glass of beer."

They walked away from the church and round two corners to the bar of the Kings. When the Sergeant stopped once, to light the pipe, Jackson said nothing. His eyes had the patient desperate hopelessness of one who had seen too many editions go to bed without the headline there could have been.

After the swing door, he steered the sergeant from the bar towards the clean-washed, bare, stale-beer-smelling tables. One was already occupied, so soon after opening time, by two men whose hunched shoulders indicated that their conversation was already far too private. Jackson went right to the far end of the low, cold room, deposited the sergeant there, and then went back to the bar, going through the motions meticulously, as though it were easier to do it that way than to rely to the slightest extent on an acquaintance of thirty years.

When he came back with the glasses, which he placed in the centre of the table indifferently, he sat looking down with a frown of pain. The sergeant wondered if Jackson had been in the wrong profession all his life, whether he should never have been a reporter and then a news editor in the first place, or whether it was just interviewing someone he knew, extracting information even from a friend who too obviously did not want to give it, that pained him.

"Are you going to make an arrest?" Jackson said at last, having evidently succeeded in summing up the quintescence of everything he needed to know in a single phrase. He did not look at the sergeant. It was evident that he believed that at that point he did not need to.

"I would," the sergeant said mildly. "I'd arrest almost anyone," he paused to drink. "Even the barman who sold this beer, if you could mention any crime."

"You know," Jackson said, grimly persevering. "You must know, or you wouldn't be there. You wouldn't have been there at all. Even knowing, I couldn't credit that you would be there. Beautiful no doubt. The only evidence of success of police methods in all your career. He not only reformed by a prison sentence but reconciled to such an extent he marries her. If he had money, of course, and she hadn't, it would be more beautiful still, if less convincing. Tolstoy wrote it, but you couldn't express it in the local paper. Only you wouldn't need actually to go to see it. Not unless you were thinking of something else."

"What are you talking about, Tip?" the sergeant said.

Jackson's dark eyes, which never seemed wholly to open or to escape from the expression of midnight sleeplessness, gave him a baleful, baffled glance, the substance of which was hopelessness.

"He raped her," he said, "in the street, some six years back. At least he did unless the names are exactly the same but the people different, which isn't likely."

The sergeant, sitting uncomfortably on the inadequate chair, to the unsteady table, surveyed his glass.

"No," he agreed judiciously, "it isn't likely. On the other hand they've got to know each other better since. Perhaps she's learned wisdom, as well as him. Or maybe they've both discovered that there is a formula by which they can repeat the action, at less than five year intervals, within the law."

"Not in the street," said Jackson. "If you had foreknowledge that they were to do it in the street, it would at least be an explanation of your presence at the wedding."

The sergeant did not answer for a little while. He was staring at the barman. When he caught the man's eye, he raised an eyebrow. It was a way of saying no to Jackson, of telling him that he had nothing to give. If he had been able to give him a phrase or two of copy, Jackson would have bought the second round.

"What are you going to do with it?" the sergeant asked. "Break it gently to the town? In view of today's wedding, it's going to take some phrasing."

"And offend all ruling families?" Jackson said. "All twenty of them? It would be a slur where it would hurt them most, on their children, who went to that

141

school. How would you like your daughter to have gone to a school run by a mistress who was not only raped but who went to the extent of proving her liking for it by marrying the man who raped her? On the other hand it's worth a column if we syndicate it to the national dailies."

Dim, the sergeant thought as the barman approached them. That was what was the matter, dim. Jackson not only knew the rules, he kept them. He ruled his area, and the only reason his nightly two pennyworth of dullness was not even duller was that something had to go in, besides births, marriages and deaths, to fill the space. But the worst of it was, his instinct was right. The ideal local rag would be a three column paper. Births in one, marriages in the next, and deaths filling all the middle of the page. If only there were enough of them, whom people knew, to make a good hour's reading over supper. Anything more than that was not merely superfluous, it was derogatory.

"Thank you, George," he said.

"Well?" he said to Jackson.

"Is it going to break?" Jackson said. "Am I going to have to report an arrest or not? Is anything likely to happen within the next six weeks?"

The sergeant said, with honest astonishment: "What the devil should I arrest him for?"

"You were there, at the wedding," Jackson said insistently.

"Do I have to be about to make an arrest, just because I look in at a local wedding?" the sergeant said.

Jackson looked bitterly at his bitter beer.

"So that's it," he said. "You don't know what is going to happen next."

"I don't know that anything is going to happen next," the sergeant said.

"Something will happen tonight," Jackson said. "But I can't report that."

He looked reconciled. The sergeant guessed, from the appearance of him, that the story would not be printed. The sergeant speculated on that fact, looking at Jackson, who was not good to look at, and seeing in him the integrity of a local press. Or at least dimness and sufficient professional despair and policy and accordance with the local standards not to print what would only be an awkward scandal in the town.

"You tell me," he said. "I thought they would be travelling tonight."

"An hotel in London," Jackson said. "They travel by air to Monaco tomorrow. Presumably, since she holds the purse strings, she was not going to have the first night in train or boat or aircraft."

"Monaco?" the sergeant said. "Is she as wealthy as that?"

"She got five thousand for the school. She paid four thousand for it five years ago, but then it was just a building and could hardly be called a school. He got a thousand for the shop, goodwill, and stock in trade. They say he paid five hundred for it a year ago. I suppose it sounds like wealth to them. Perhaps they've convinced themselves they're financial wizards. Anyway, it's Monaco, the Grand Hotel."

"Do you think he's mad?" the sergeant said.

"So that's what you went there to see? If he or she or which of them was mad?"

They looked at one another. Their thoughts were on a man called Harold Clemens.

They did not know him, the sergeant thought.

But there were three of them now, watching him. Jackson, the bank manager, and himself. In time, there might be more. It seemed most likely that he could get away with nothing.

# CHAPTER FIFTEEN

IMPLACABLE, Clem thought. If only he could think of himself as implacable and not as hunted, haunted. He sat on the terrace at the little table with the small glass of white wine before him. He shifted his gaze from the impossible blue of the Mediterranean to the little harbour and thence to the crowded, dusty, hot and noisy roadway that lay immediately below him. He was conscious that on his left the middle-aged Frenchman and the startling, stunning girl, who looked sixteen, a French sixteen, an age which had nothing to do with youth or innocence, were rising and moving off. The waiter, seeing them go, came out with his tray and cloth and removed their glasses and wiped their table. He saw the French couple descend the steps and reach the road. There were other girls there, equally clothed, enhanced and draped and underlined by clothing, with a sophistication that gave purpose to every scrap of lace and button, not decorated, certainly not covered by it, but declaring loudly their self-advertisement. Even a woman of forty, unmarried perhaps, perhaps divorced, with a man of sixty at her side. What fashion could do with a figure that was guarded with complete absorption and intensity through every moment of every day.

Perhaps a half of the people within his range of vision, which included a mile or more of streets and the harbour and the yachts, were there on a honeymoon of some kind, even if for some it was the perpetual honeymoon, the lifelong residence on the coast, the physical reality of the scene a refuge, for those who could afford it, from that darker unreality, that nightmare world of factory and street and cloud and rain and unending twilight that stretched northwards all the way to the British Isles. For them the facts of life, the naked facts. He saw one girl, alone, her body brown and nearly naked, walking from nowhere to nowhere on the street. She was: she existed as a totality, as an expression of the present moment, among the people who were dressed. Not since Roman times had the present moment existed, so brazen, pure, and clear, so divorced from what had gone and what was still to come. She defeated time, that tall lithe girl, not only for herself, not even particularly for herself, but for every man, however distant, into whose range of vision she might stray. Like a jewel, like one of the rubies or diamonds the older women wore, she was a concentration of intensity, complete in herself, without relevance forward or backwards or to either side: unlike, Clem thought, that night three nights ago in the hotel in London.

The scene, his scene, the one in which he lived, was enclosed, quite suddenly, in a total cloud. Memory obscured it, memory which restricted itself, in darkness and artificial light, to a single room, a bed. So that was what she had wanted. That was the image that had lived in her mind through all her barren years, fulfilled by him, actualised at last in that room and bed. Had he damned himself utterly by giving it to her; was he defiled? The cloud dispersed. He was back in the actual scene again, present at the terrace table with the wine before him. If there had been defilement, he thought, it pertained only to the place : that that should happen there. Here, the sunlight was a sterilising force, burning up all evil vapours, so that what happened, no matter what it was, was rendered pagan and actual but limited to itself. Truth, and not morality, was visible in the white dust on the sunlit terrace steps.

Today, he thought. It must be today. He had fulfilled her. There was no future for her, no further way or direction for her to go. He had been scrupulously careful in his justice.

The sunlight glittered on the harbour, and in the sea breeze a white sail slowly flapped, folding itself through its own translucent shadows.

She came, emerging from the dark doorway past the waiter and padding towards him between the tables. She was undressed now, and too visibly skin and bone, the pale skin pink with sunburn, the breadth of the hips all bone beneath the circle of cloth she wore like a shameless hussy, the breasts certainly not worth the thin slackness of the brassiere the thighs unpleasant with a tactile roughness. But most naked of all was her self-complacent grin, of a vanity unbelievable in that scene.

He rose. He finished his wine as he stood up. He put out his hand to hers, deliberate and unflinching, without a tremor revealing his intention so much as to create the need to mask it. She believed. She believed in herself. She saw no impossibility, nothing wrong in her imagination that he loved her. He said :

"You're here. I'm glad. Come. You may not like it, but at least we'll try it once."

"You know me now," she said, looking deliberately

and with unnecessary shamelessness into his eyes. "You ought to by now. I'll try anything once."

The waiter, Clem saw, looking behind her, was bored. He too saw no incongruity in the love. He had seen stranger sights every day, and did not speculate. For a moment, for just one strange instant, Clem wondered whether he did not in fact love her after all, impossible and senseless as his mind and all his senses told him that that was. He understood her. He saw that clearly. He understood her as no one else did. Was it credible that, understanding, he also did not disapprove of her? Further, that he appreciated her, her every truly childlike, imaginedly knowing, whim and gesture? His brain took over again. He could not love her. It was a sheer impossibility. They moved away from the table, and he kept her hand as they moved down the steps.

She liked to parade herself all but nakedly through the streets, she who in her former existence had never come anywhere near to doing that. He had fulfilled her indeed, and taught her to give expression to her wishes. In fact it was only her feelings that were aroused by their progress through the hot sunlight on the pavement by the roadway. When they pushed their way through a group by a stopped car she did not even cause a turning of the heads. She was immersed, as in a fluid, in the total indifference of the Monaco crowd, and therefore not only shameless but permitted to be shameless. How rash, he thought, for her to expose her skin to the light again. He thought of stopping, of insisting that she go back for a wrap, but decided that she would never feel the pain. He coolly decided not to complicate her last moments for her and was astonished at the clarity of his thinking.

"Which quay?" she said interestedly, seeing the harbour before them.

He relinquished her hand and took her arm: "This way."

The café people looked idly down at them as they passed. The basic fact of life at Monaco was that parade. One watched or one paraded; the roles were interchangeable. But no one penetrated beyond the painter's preoccupation with the impact of mere images on the senses. The fish in the acquarium had the same appeal exactly, as moving shapes and colours, but they lacked the clarity of the sunlight, the possibility of arousing desires, impersonal desires, such as might be aroused by a book of nudes, as well. The people on the café terraces above them talked about their own concerns.

"Here," he said, as the quay stretched before them with its boats, the water faded and darker now when seen from a different angle, the blinding white dust, and the white sail flapping.

At his side, she walked along the quay with that careful deliberation of thighs and hips which all her life formerly had been concealed inside a dress.

A Frenchman in blue, his trousers faded and too short, his wrinkled face grinning, came towards them.

"Madame will see if she likes it," Clem said with self-conscious jocularity, finding no need to act a part. He had no need to pretend to be himself. He was himself, even to his inadequate French which made him speak, with a hint of shame, in English, which the Frenchman did not understand. It was the basic situation of Monaco, the intimate understanding barred by a language difference yet finding expression still through manner and visual movement.

"Deux heurs?" the Frenchman said, grinning at them understandingly because they stood close together. Clem found his arm released. She left him and went to the edge of the quay and stood there looking at the boats.

"Which is ours?" she asked.

"I don't know," Clem said. "The little one with the sail up I presume. I asked him this morning, but neither he nor I were clear."

He had taken out his wallet and was offering money. The Frenchman, having received no answer to his query as to how long, waved the money back good-naturedly.

"That's all very well," Clem said, deliberately playing a part this time, "but I'd know better how long we could afford if I knew how much an hour."

He put his money away however, and pointed to the boat, the one with the sail. The Frenchman nodded emphatically and indicated that it was quite his.

They got aboard. It was a little yacht, more delicate in construction than the fishing boats but with faded paint and with a lack of varnish on the seats and coamings. It had none of the splendour of the private yachts, not even the tiniest ones, of which the largest, with its towering mast, could have carried a dozen on its deck. Their boat looked like what it was, one of the very few, perhaps the only one, which someone found it worthwhile to hire out to tourists.

She was climbing aft along the deck and laughing uncertainly as it rocked beneath her. The sail, the movements of which had seemed so slow when seen from a distance, now flapped and heeled the boat with a hint of danger.

Clem wished he knew more about sailing. It was certainly part of his plan that he should not know, having only what intelligence and close observation could teach him. Yet he had to repress the glittering excitement of his eye, conscious as he was of the danger of mere physical and mechanical failure, due to mere lack of aptitude.

"The first thing we do is hoist the foresail," he said. "Then we cast off, and her head swings round, and we sail away."

"As long as you know how to bring us back," she said. She was sitting down uncertainly in the stern and holding on, her head ducked beneath the topped-up boom, obviously very conscious of the water that was only inches from her.

He said nothing, the time being past for speech now. He hoisted the foresail clumsily under the eyes of a little collecting crowd. He had nothing to fear from their witnessing of his seamanship. The sail blew about him as he made the halyard fast; undignified, obviously incompetent, he had to fight it to try to reach the bow-line.

Someone called out to him and stooped to the ring on the quay. He tumbled aft. In fact, he had sailed once previously, on a reservoir, the right amount of experience exactly for his purpose. He knew enough to cast off, but hold on to, the stern line that held them to another boat.

Not only did the man on the quay cast them off, but he gave the bow a pull in the right direction before he threw the line on board. For a moment they went off dangerously until Clem got the foresail sheeted in, the mainsheet slack, and the helm hard over. They made a broad reach for the harbour entrance, the breeze gusty beneath the wall and the boat heeling and coming upright again. Someone shouted to them from the quay. It was the boom, which was still topped up. Clem let it stay. He hoped they would clear the corner.

The little crowd on the quay began to move slowly seawards, to watch them. They were something to see: an English couple who would probably make fools of themselves doing something no Frenchman would do unless he were fully expert.

Above them in the sunlight the town looked down. They must be visible, Clem knew, from a hundred cafés, from the streets. He came out of the shelter of the wall now and mercifully the breeze was slack. They moved out into the brighter glitter of the open sea. Hundreds more people must be able to see them at every moment.

"It's only getting under way that's difficult," he said. "We can relax now and sail where we like. The sea is ours."

She was taking to it uncomfortably. She had been scared, sensing lack of control, as they left the harbour. They sailed peacefully on the open sea for half an hour. At the end of that time, she was sitting up on the sidedeck with him, beginning, with her childlike innocence, and newly discovered delight in small things, to take more pleasure.

He brought her down into the well of the boat and came about carefully, heading out to sea. They would be small now, a white pyramid only, seen from the town. He brought her up onto the side-deck again, inviting her to sit beside him and hold the foresheet.

They sailed for another half hour before he slacked all sheets and turned for home, drifting downwind in a state that seemed utterly peaceful and secure.

He watched the mainsail and judged the direction of the wind. He looked up at the town that lay before them. It was inevitable that they should gybe around the harbour wall, and he could see the heads there, the people with nothing to do but watch. Not too near, he thought. He came on the wind a little, a course that would force the gybe on him a little farther out. Perhaps a hundred thousand people would see him do it.

"Don't you find this pleasant?" he asked her.

For some reason her eyes were scared now, and she did not answer. He went forward and lowered the boom.

After twenty minutes he said: "Keep still. I have to sail dead down wind now, almost in the direction of the wind itself." The boat was upright, and seemed stable, and there could be nothing, to her eyes, to be alarmed about. Her woman's world, her whole life, had been lived in a state of sublime innocence of all mechanical forces.

A few more people were drifting out to the pier end. They saw him sailing a little by the lee, trying to make the harbour without the gybe. Perhaps in some café far above them some retired colonel would have the glasses on him, saying: "That's very clever or very ignorant sailing. With that woman on the side-deck, the man's either an expert or a fool."

He brought the tiller over very gently when they were still a hundred yards away from the nearest watchers. No gaze, however intent, could have seen the motion of his hand. The air became fluky near the harbour. The sail quivered, then settled back again.

Suddenly, there was no wind to fill the sail. The boat began to tilt with the unbalanced weight upon the sidedeck. When the breeze came again, it was behind the sail. The sail, the boom, came across quite slowly. There was no instant whipping or desperate action. The boat capsized, heeling to the point when water was entering the centre well. The boom caught Emma Clemens across the face, forcing her almost gently, but quite firmly, off and backwards, downwards, in one straight slide into the water.

Clem called. He stood up in the boat, on the stern, as it righted itself. He was looking aft. He could be seen to be looking aft by all the town. He did what every young man on honeymoon, every inexpert sailor would do. He dived into the sea, into the cool, sunlit ocean.

A hundred thousand faces in the town were suddenly intent, watching, wondering if there was any danger, seeing the boat sail on, turn sharply, come up into the wind with no one at the tiller, pay off, sail off again, and come up into the wind again.

Clem could be seen in the water swimming weakly, with a breast stroke, in circles. They could see him holding something, struggling, then he swam alone again.

The movement of the boats in the harbour seemed almost leisurely. Engines had to be started and ropes cast off. The shouts of the people at the end of the quay were not at first understood by those who were farther inland. There was a tendency at first for everyone to look round in the expectation that someone else was doing something. One man in particular had to be convinced before he suddenly turned and ran along the quay and jumped into his boat. It was the boat-owner, the Frenchman in blue, and the craft he chose to go out in was a rowing skiff.

One engine burst into a full throated roar, then suddenly died. A man began to work furiously on it, then looked round to see if anyone else would get there first. When the Frenchman in his skiff emerged from the harbour he started off directly for his escaping boat. He had to be called back and directed to where Clem swam.

No less than three motor boats emerged together. They circled in a splother of foam. One of them picked Clem up and they went on circling. The Frenchman began to row after his boat again. The crowd watched him because no sooner did he near the boat than she started away again, like a skittish wild thing, waiting for him and then sailing out of his reach, and steadily getting away from where the boats were circling, circling monotonously now and very slowly.

Two boats went back, and one of them lay there, alone, rocking in the swell, everyone standing or sitting on it and looking at the sea, the empty glittering sea below the harbour wall.

The figure of a hundred thousand was an exaggeration, Clem realised, thinking slowly to himself, standing on the side of the boat and looking at the sea immediately before him. That must be about the total population of the town. But ten or twenty thousand must have seen it, in broad daylight, in the clearest sunlight in the middle of the afternoon. He thought wearily that there would have to be an inquest.

## CHAPTER SIXTEEN

IT was comparatively rare in the sergeant's experience that he was able to collect the evidence for a crime before it happened. Even the evidence of crimes in the past sometimes came to him in devious ways.

It was raining in Eventham. There was rain on the shoulders of the sergeant's civilian coat and on his soft hat when he went in. He noticed the rain drops on the coats of the two clients before him when he stood waiting before the counter in the mellow light. They watched, all of them, the back of the other client, the one who had the attention of the clerk, seeing not exactly with indifference the piles of notes, the copper and silver that were being shovelled on the counter into little bags.

The clerk looked up. Perhaps it was to see how many were standing waiting for his attention perhaps it was the reflex action of a bank clerk. He must have seen, the sergeant thought, that there were three waiting at his particular section of the counter, and no one lurking in the shadows. But his gaze settled for an instant on the sergeant.

"The manager would like a word with you, Mr. Huntley." His words were barely audible. His eyes hardly met those of the sergeant for an instant. He resumed his counting of the bank notes.

So, the sergeant thought.

He moved quietly along the counter. He did not

ask for attention but stood contentedly in the deeper light beyond the other clerks at the farther end. In time a door opened, preceeded by a shadow that fell on frosted glass.

No apparent contact or recognition passed between the sergeant and the manager. At one moment the manager was holding his door open, well-mannered, showing a client out, and the next he was standing there, in the same position, but holding the door for the sergeant to go in.

It was brighter, quieter, in the smooth, calm office. They sat on each side of the polished desk.

"You don't actually go out and walk a beat in this weather, do you?" the manager asked in passive, idle curiosity.

"Sometimes," the sergeant said comfortably. "Sometimes I do it when you're safely tucked in bed."

The manager regarded the phenomenon with interest.

"You'll be all the more pleased to retire then," he said.

The sergeant looked at him. He said: "I wondered if it was that." His expression was a denial of his words.

"It isn't only our major clients we take an interest in," the manager said defensively. "For example, it's a year since you completed those payments on—"

The manager had forgotten.

"You've said that before," the sergeant said. "Besides, it wasn't one year ago. It was two. My financial position is sound, but it isn't interesting."

The manager sighed. He said: "There was another little thing."

The sergeant had thought there was, but he did not go so far as to say so.

The manager moved. Since he had not shown specific approval before, his expression could hardly be described as disapproval now, though it was apparent that he had an attitude to what he had to say.

"It was some time ago," he said with a distinct idleness of tone, "that we had a talk about a man called Clemens."

The sergeant still sat motionless. If there was some subtle difference in his attitude, it was not perceptible.

"It's surprising how quickly some people can make money," said the manager fussily. "I think you remarked on that."

The manager picked up a pencil from his desk and began to play with it. The sergeant watched him.

"I don't think I remarked on how quickly people make money," the sergeant said. "I think I was concerned then with what he had, not what he was going to make."

"It's the same thing," the manager said.

The sergeant studied the manager carefully. He could see there was a difficulty. It was too obvious for him not to be aware of it.

"I think I tried to help you when he came to you as an unknown customer from the outside," he said.

The manager looked at the sergeant with bright, wide eyes.

"I don't think people would approve of our helping one another," he said.

The sergeant considered the problem. Clemens had been married the previous week.

"He started with five hundred," he said. "What has he got now?"

The manager simply looked at him.

"Do you think I can tell you what a client has in his account?"

"If you're not going to do that," the sergeant said, "I don't see that you can tell me anything at all."

"He's been making money very quickly," the manager said as a great concession. "Especially when he sold his business."

The sergeant considered the manager. Of such a man he could not consider that he would be ignorant of the local gossip.

"Has he been getting it from his wife?" he said.

"No," said the manager. "That is, I can't tell you that."

The manager appeared to believe that he had gone as far as he could go.

The sergeant did not feel inclined to leave it just like that.

"He started with five hundred," he said. "It's reasonable that he should have made a thousand pounds."

The manager hopelessly shook his head.

"Five thousand?" the sergeant said. "Ten thousand? Twenty thousand?"

"The middle," the manager said.

The sergeant nodded. His expression of silent satisfaction indicated that he was ready now to get up and go.

"It would be convenient," he said mildly, "if I knew I had got within five hundred or five thousand, but there it is."

The manager struggled with himself. "Within hundreds," he said. "Sergeant—"

"Yes?"

The manager had got up to show the sergeant out. The sergeant too had risen, but he turned again.

"Have you thought of the question why the figure should suddenly appear?"

The manager went quickly to the door and opened it.

All the sergeant could say was "Thank you."

"Don't mention it," the manager said; but he attached an unusual degree of meaning to the words.

The sergeant went out into the rain, forgetting his business at the counter, pondering the significance of the manager's final question.

Why should the figure suddenly appear? Why should a man wish to, need to, enter his wealth in a bank account and make it quite official? It was as interesting as the question of why he had not done so earlier.

If Clemens wished to live abroad, for instance. It would not be easy to smuggle ten thousand pounds. But when he had last spoken to Emma Smith she had not said anything about going to live abroad.

The sergeant was making his way to the police station. At the police station it might be possible to answer the other question. If a man had not entered his money earlier it could only be because he had not had it or because he had not wished it to be known he had it. But no one in the immediate locality, to the sergeant's certain knowledge, had reported the sudden loss of ten thousand pounds, or even nine thousand.

It was possible that at the police station he would discover that someone, somewhere, but not too far away, and not outside specific dates, had lost such a sum. He almost hoped he would not do that. If Clemens were a criminal from the first it would affect the attitude he had taken to his conversations with Emma Smith. It would distinctly affect the somewhat absent and negative assurances he had given her.

Despite the early hour the street lamps were on and the sergeant, with his hat tipped down against the rain, was navigating as it were by their reflections on the wet pavements. He was conscious of a shadow which he dodged but which did not go away.

It was Jackson, Jackson in a much-used raincoat, sardonic, and confronting him.

"Sergeant, the very man!" said Jackson.

The sergeant stopped, but the very last thing he wished to do was to discuss the case with Jackson.

"He's done it," Jackson said, indifferent to the drizzle and the lowering weather, as though his normal habitat was the streets.

The sergeant stared. He had an impulse to ask who had done what. He repressed it. Jackson, he was more than conscious, would tell him all the same.

"From Monaco," Jackson said, retailing the most striking news for many a year. "We had an Agency wire." Jackson's face contorted. "Tragic Death of Local Bride on Honeymoon—Husband's Heroic Efforts from Capsized Boat." Jackson suddenly wore a changed expression.

"What are you telling me, Jackson?"

"An item of local news," Jackson said. He stood theatrically, but did not laugh.

"Is that all you have? Is that how you're going to print it?"

"How else, Sergeant?" Jackson said, staring at him coldly. "You want us to send a reporter there to get

161

the proof? To Monaco where they do their best to avoid a scandal? He's not a fool, Sergeant, but—"

Jackson's tone changed. Softly, he said :

"Sergeant, he's made a fool of you."

The sergeant's face went red.

Jackson turned, melting into the growing dusk. The sergeant saw him cross the road and enter a lighted doorway, like a shadow across the glistening street. If the sergeant had followed Jackson, he could be sure, he would find him propped against a bar where someone, even out of hours, would be serving him the first of the evening drinks.

The sergeant was not unaware that the fact that Jackson should do it, openly and defiantly, was an expression of Jackson's opinion of the sergeant. But Jackson, the sergeant remembered, did not know the whole story. Had Jackson known it all, he might have carried his imputation further, beyond the accusation of incompetence, to the statement that the sergeant had caused the death of Emma Smith, and not merely that, because of that incompetence, he had permitted it.

The sergeant turned quickly on his heel. There was no one to see the violence of his anger as he began to walk again. He went on to the police station, to discover who, and where, and when, had lost a sum that he now evaluated as almost exactly nine thousand pounds.

# CHAPTER SEVENTEEN

"**D**O you like this place?" the sergeant said, leaning over the low barrier of plants in boxes and speaking to the lone man at the table.

The scene was in the Piazza della Signoria in Florence and the time was one year later. The café by some legalistic process the sergeant wholly failed to understand, had appropriatd a specific portion of the square. Not only did its chairs and tables block the pavement, so that pedestrians strolling from the fashionable shopping streets to the Uffizi gallery must run the gauntlet of obstructions and mingle with the waiters with their silver trays, but it had also erected barriers, rendered semi-permanent by the plants in tubs and boxes that adorned them, to mark off an appreciable area of the roadway.

Clem turned and recognised the arrival of the sergeant while the sergeant watched him.

There was no doubt, the sergeant thought, that both the café itself, and the facilities it offered, improved the scene. Without it, the square would have been too large, too bare, too businesslike, despite the line of white marble statues, surely the nudest male nudes in all the world, that culminated in the erotic Neptune fountain and marked off the limits of traffic circulation on the farther side. The sergeant was almost sure that the frowning walls there were those of the Palazzo Vecchio. Across the corner the area with the covering roof was the loggis in which the famous sculptures were presented, so that the women sitting knitting in the sunlight on the steps had behind them the magnificent and realistic representation of the Rape of their Sabine forbears. But the sergeant was not primarily interested in the classical antiquities or the Renaissance. He was watching Clem, watching the eyes that first widened and then narrowed as they saw him, watching the gap that preceeded any words at all.

"Why, Sergeant," Clem said. "What brings you so far?"

His gaze was distant, the sergeant saw. And then he saw the strange smile dawning, a smile of poise and curious interest. If the sergeant had had to find a word for it, he would have said that there was something mathematical about the smile.

The sergeant was not unduly slow. He simply stood, for an adequate time, to allow his presence to register on the other. "My wife," he then said, "is shopping." And that, he seemed to imply, was an adequate explanation of his presence there, if not for his arrival in the city.

Clem accepted the explanation, apparently the whole of it, including the implication of time to spare. Indeed he could hardly not do so since the other places were vacant at his table. He allowed his eyes to move to a vacant chair. It was an invitation, though how willing the sergeant could not guess.

The last thing there could be in such a place was hurry. The sergeant continued to stand for a moment on the wrong side of the barrier of the plants, perhaps to discover, to give Clem time to say, if he were waiting for someone else. When no such information was forthcoming, he turned and walked away.

Clem watched him go, saw him turn at the tubbed bush in the corner. He even lost sight of him for a moment behind the leaves. Then he saw him again, making towards the café entrance. The sergeant turned inwards at the pavement gap, at the café entrance, and came stalking towards Clem through the vacant tables. He arrived and pulled out, and sat down upon, the facing chair. Somehow he conveyed a distinct impression. The sergeant had arrived.

Clem looked at him with the same smile of curious interest and detachment.

"On holiday," the sergeant said, as though that were not obvious, as though he needed to be believed.

Clem registered the statement though perhaps not to the required extent. He did what was necessary.

"Have you decided what you drink in this country?" Clem said.

The waiter approached. The sergeant withdrew his gaze, which had been searching around the square. He addressed the waiter. "Coffee," he said in English. It was impossible to guess whether he had interpreted Clem's question as an offer to buy him a drink. If he had, it was at least possible that he had refused it.

Then the sergeant looked round at the square again. But he was not exactly searching for his absent wife. He would not have found her on the clean white table cloth which he apparently admired, nor among the flowers in boxes that limited the area of the café to a corner of the square. He interested himself for a moment in the statues, the spectacular white ones beneath the farther frowning walls, the Neptune fountain, and those that were almost behind him, in the open-fronted loggia, where every human passion was tranquilly immortalised in bronze and permanent stone, and a few that were not human, that could only be the transcendental passions and actions of the Gods.

"You live here?" he remarked to Clem.

Clem faced him, deliberate if with a shade more coolness and reserve behind his smile. "I live here modestly," he said. "I don't quite rate a villa at Fiesole."

The sergeant paused. He looked again across the square, perhaps actually looking for his wife on this occasion. His eyes shifted back to Clem. "I suppose I ought to express my condolences," he said steadily, as though it had been something coming all along, "on the death of Mrs. Clemens."

It was as though an object had been taken out and laid on the table between them, where they could see it.

Clem looked at him quietly and coolly, with the clarity, if not quite the coolness of the great marble statues across the square. He did not show whether he had expected the assault to be so direct.

"People have almost stopped awakening my feelings by reminding me of it," he said.

The sergeant looked at him steadily.

"You mean it belongs to the forgotten past?"

Clem returned his glance.

"I shall not forget it," he said. "I assure you of that."

There was something decisive about their mutual attitude. It was a beginning at least, an acknowledgement of the angle of the sun or of the bearing of a distant coast, an almost physical definitiveness that is to say, of their knowing where they were.

The sergeant unlocked his gaze again towards the square. "So now you live here permanently," he almost idly said. He seemed struck by the word he had inadvertently added to what had been the statement. "Permanently?" he repeated, questioning whether it were true or not.

Clem too looked across the square. Facing him was the David and the greater statues. On his right was the loggia of the Uffizi, and it was on that, or on one of the statues that stood under cover in it, that his gaze rested, for an instant almost oblivious of the sergeant.

"I feel something sympathetic here," he dryly said, not committing himself, after that moment in which his eyes had rested on a single one of the collection of graceful and famous and perfect sculptures.

It was not irrelevant that the sergeant did not turn to see on what his gaze had rested. Perhaps he had seen it already, and in any event he was looking in the other direction across the square. He believed that, in the distance, he could see his wife.

"Interpol has a line on you," he interposed, as though that had relevance to the project of living in one place or another. He did not look at Clem.

Clem sat very still. It was no news to him that Interpol, that telegraphic network of the European police, would be watching him and know exactly where he was, and would be waiting, perhaps with infinite patience, for him to marry again and drown another wife. He had lived with that and knew precisely where there was and was not danger. But that the sergeant should say it was partly another matter, just as it was that he himself, the sergeant, should have appeared in Florence.

"Sergeant," he said after a little pause. "Is any purpose served by your talking in this way?"

The sergeant reflected. "There is," he said, casual but definitive and decisive. "My wife is over there. In a little while, when she shops a little nearer, I will have to go across and speak to her."

"Your mention of Interpol is intended to tell me that it would be pointless for me to take advantage of your absence to leave this table and go away?"

"The table," said the sergeant mildly, watching his wife, "or the city."

"But do you think that that will discourage me from abandoning a conversation that might be unpleasant and need not be prolonged?"

"I think it should," the sergeant as calmly said.

Clem sat passively and physically at ease. It was clear that he refused to burden himself with anxieties that had no known source.

The sergeant turned to him. "I could have you arrested for the Hapton crime," he said. "It's only a matter of extradition. I will have you arrested for the Hapton crime."

Clem's physical attitude was unchanged. It would have been impossible for a physiologist to show that he had moved a single muscle. But perhaps that was precisely it. Such complete immobility was no longer relaxation. It was a form of sudden tension.

"For that crime," the sergeant said idly, with a gloss over the implication that there were several, "it would have been easier to extradite you than to come to see you. I think you should be interested in why I have not done so so far."

He turned back to examine the further movements

of his wife, who indeed was coming straight towards them.

He rose from his chair and moved a little backwards from the table.

"I'll have a word with her," he calmly said. "I know she would prefer to continue her shopping. I don't think you will want to meet her. You may prefer to think of what I've said for a little while, but I don't think you'd be wise to go away."

Clem's smile was still there but somewhat frozen. He made no attempt to accompany the sergeant when he went away. He went on sitting at the table, and the sergeant, looking back at him for an instant as he left the café, thought he was thinking of the detail and digesting what he had said.

He was mistaken.

The flowers in the boxes round the café had a sun-faded and almost absent scent. So barely perceptible was the smell of them that Clem had not noticed it before. But now he did notice it, and, since he noticed it, it reminded him somehow suddenly and inexplicably of his late wife. He was conscious of the scent of the flowers as almost a pervading continuance of the spirit of Emma Smith, who was one year dead.

# CHAPTER EIGHTEEN

THE sergeant returned, crossing the square again in the sunlight and out of sunlight into shade, pausing to look at the statues in the Uffizi loggia, and then entering the café again, stalking through the lines of tables, and seating himself once more, deliberately, in the empty chair.

They remained silent for a moment, while he looked round at the peaceful scene and then at Clem.

"This," he remarked, "is better than an English gaol."

The remark was so cool and factual that it might have passed as a piece of ordinary conversation, of banter between friends.

Clem regarded the sergeant closely. He seemed to hesitate, as though he had something to say but did not know whether to say it yet or not. He decided to say it.

"I have no great love for an English gaol," he said. "What struck me about an English gaol was that the punishment was so unequal."

The sergeant leant towards the table. "Is this irrelevant?"

"You should know it is not irrelevant," Clem said. "You mentioned it. And it is not irrelevant that prison is hardly punishment at all for the very idle. You can remember I have been there. It is hardly a punishment for the miserable or depraved." He looked at the sergeant a moment longer and introduced more meaning into his voice.

"Some things were unspeakable," he said. "Little things. Little to you. Using a toilet after forty others who did not know how or did not wish to use it. The punishment of a civilised country. No toilet paper. The kind of incidents that can be treated as a joke the first time. Some people accept damp grey walls and make no distinction between these buildings and this square here and that architecture of the damned. Only it just so happened that for me the idleness and the architecture, and the lack of sanitation, and the company of those who did not mind them—particularly the company I had to live with in the cells—was a kind of specific torture. I don't exaggerate. The unadulterated waste of time alone might have been designed expressly as a punishment—a punishment for someone who before he went to gaol had been conscious of time, and anxious to get on, and had never wasted a single moment."

The waiter was approaching them, bearing a fresh cup of coffee that Clem had ordered, convincingly, or else deliberately, as an evidence of his calmness.

"You have strong feelings," the sergeant said.

Clem watched the waiter approach and watched the sergeant sit back in his chair as the waiter served him.

"I have," Clem said. "I even think I have a right to have them. And it's not irrelevant to what you said before you went away."

The sergeant nodded. It was he who now watched Clem being served. "You're probably wondering why I came here."

Clem looked at him steadily even before the waiter left.

"You said you were on holiday, and then you said something else. I would rather believe the former."

The sergeant had discovered the sugar in the saucer of his coffee cup and was carefully unwrapping the wrapped cubes with blunt fingers. He looked up.

"There are a number of places I could have gone on holiday. A sergeant on a sergeant's pay doesn't usually come as far as this." Holding the sugar, he paused for a moment. "Have you ever thought why I am a sergeant"

Clem considered it as though he, now, were wondering at the relevance.

"No," he said. "I haven't thought why you are still a sergeant."

The sergeant accepted the implied compliment impassively. In a sense, he even exceeded it.

"There have to be some wise, or intelligent, or knowing sergeants," he said. "Men who keep their ear to the ground. Who know what is going on."

Clem found no answer to the suggestion that the sergeant knew what was going on.

The sergeant did not relax his gaze. "Much of what I hear is gossip of course," he said. "Some of it isn't. Some of it is evidence. Some of it is evidence that can't be used. But the man who has to listen also has to think. He has to sort out one kind from the other. And even when there is no evidence, he still may hear something that will tell him where to look for evidence. I spend a lot of time doing that. Hearing gossip, and sorting it, and looking for evidence that does not exist."

The sergeant dropped the sugar in the centre of his coffee cup.

Clem showed minor signs of strain. He had begun well enough. He had been at least as poised as the sergeant had ever been, and he had even recovered from a setback while the sergeant had been away, but now the strain was showing in a minor deviation, a not-completely-perfect guarding of his tone.

"You've come here?" he said. "To confess to me?" He laughed sharply.

The sergeant answered with a look.

"You'd be surprised how near you are," he said deliberately. "It's so near to a confession, what I'm telling you. It's a problem, Clemens. A problem you have posed me. Do you know you've given me a wealth of trouble? I told you Interpol had a line on you, but a sergeant can't just call on the services of Interpol to find a man. It's more usual to have a reason. It was just that something—this problem—intervened. To have given the reason as it stood would have made it unnecessary for me to come here at all. It would have amounted to prejudgment. I'll tell you, but you'll have to hear it."

Clem was surprisingly still now as he looked at him. It was the sergeant who was playing with the coffee. Clem's stood as it had been, and the sergeant did not look at his.

"You gave me your opinion of prison," the sergeant said. "I sympathise with you. I wouldn't be here if I didn't sympathise. But there's something else. There's the question not only of the punishment but the justice. You may say it isn't a sergeant's business to think of justice, and you would be right. A sergeant or any other policeman. His business is to look at the crime, collect the evidence, and arrest a likely man. Just as Counsel's business is to make out a case. And a judge's business is to administer the law. And a jury's business is to look at the evidence and on that alone decide who did the crime. But I don't work that way. That is my failing, that justice means something else to me."

Clem's eyes were fixed on him. "It's a little idle to talk of justice," Clem said. "What you are talking about is the machinery of the law."

"Because," said the sergeant, "there's nothing in that system that seeks to do justice to, or even begins with a consideration of, the man? I've told you. I listen to gossip. I talk to people. I'm useful in that. I am useful to my superiors. But also it allows me to do a little justice to the man."

"At the expense," Clem said, "of the rapidity of your promotion? Is that the point?"

"It might be the point," the sergeant said. "It might be a help to my promotion, if it isn't too late for that, *if* I had you arrested for the Hapton crime. Only I've not done it. If you want a point, you can find it perhaps in that."

He leaned forward and leant one elbow on the table, closing as it were, and coming abruptly nearer.

"You're going to have to talk to me, Clemens," he said quietly but intently, and with a fine-drawn tension. "It isn't that I need any tips, because you know I know. It isn't a question of the evidence, because I have the evidence now. There's a file in my office ... A file that only has to go forward to send you up to Dartmoor, to put it indelicately, for a nine-year stretch. At least. Why I don't use that evidence and send you there is another matter. Why I haven't used it yet, that is. Maybe that is the point, the nature of my finer ethics. Ethics that even you are going to have to understand, just because I have that feeling that it's necessary to do justice to the man. To the man. You follow me? And not therefore about the Hapton crime at all. The other thing, beside the Hapton crime. That's in the balance. They call it murder. You can see how that will sway a man of the finest ethic. As long as the murder is there, you can see I'm out to get you with no holds barred. And the Hapton crime is useful. The Hapton crime is only useful. I can use it as a lever."

The sergeant stopped, facing Clem and looking at him intently, and they sat there quietly in the café surrounded by the faint but persistent, the hardly detectable scent of the flowers.

# CHAPTER NINETEEN

THE sergeant, Clem suddenly realised, was a sadist. More than anything that was the explanation for his presence in the town of Florence.

The sun had come round a little and was now shining brightly on the clean white tablecloth, on the two of them, the café and the square. Since the morning air was cool and the café was resting in its out-of-season peace, they might on some other occasion, or had they been other people, have remarked on the heightened sensibility their surroundings gave them. But they were only two men leaning forward, intent upon one another across a table, finding privacy, not peace, preoccupation and concentration, not distraction, in their sunlit isolation in the empty square.

Clem made an effort and smiled. "Sergeant," he said, and now it was an effort. "It isn't only that I don't know what you're talking about!" The effort was still there, even in the need to say it. "Even if what you say were true—and I deny it—I doubt if you have any evidence to connect me with any crime at all!"

It was brave, since Clem could not disguise or deny that the sergeant had mentioned the town, the right town, Hapton, the very name of which he had not expected to find associated with himself.

But perhaps he knew. Perhaps it was desperation, since he must have known by then that the sergeant would not have come so far and said so much if he had not had something. And if he had not known before, he must have known then, to see the sergeant still regarding him closely, intently but unhurried, appreciatively but undisturbed.

The sergeant even picked up his coffee cup. "You're an unlucky man, Clemens," he said almost idly as he sipped it, with that apparent idleness which was not in fact an idleness of any kind. "I seem to remember that some years ago there was a particular outcry against what they then called sex-crimes. I wonder how much you keep in touch with news from home? If you do, you'll know that the swing has gone the other way. It's the man with the cosh who gets the maximum sentence now. Almost as much as he would for murder. You know how it is. They attach so much significance to a word. It's always the same man apparently, whether he cracks a female skull to take a handbag or relieves a bank messenger in Hapton and very carefully does not kill him. They behave as though he killed him. Since capital punishment was repealed, there is very little difference."

Clem did not go pale. At that point his attitude was still that all the sergeant said was make-believe and lies. But he was insistent to a point he would not have been had he been able to retain his original air of total lack of interest.

"What was this crime at Hapton?" he very deliberately said, the irrelevance of the question quite spoiled by the air with which he asked it.

The sergeant answered him to begin with with a steady look. It was a look that indicated that the answer, the answer to the question behind the question, would not come in words. But then he embarked on an action that did far more than answer it.

He watched Clem watch his hand as it left the table and went towards his inner pocket. His movements were deliberate but not unduly slow. He watched Clem's eyes watch as the hand reappeared, bearing two photographs or something similar, wondering whether Clem already recognised the prison record photographs of himself.

Then, with a directness that went considerably further than the question, he handed the photographs across.

Clem took them, but there was now some uncertainty about the way he took them, as though even then he were calculating the possibility that he might refuse them or deny them, as though something could be gained by that. But he took them, even in initial ignorance of what they were, though seeing they were photographs of himself.

Clem examined them. As photographs they were identical, as identical with one another as they must be with the original, and from the same negative as the original in the Criminal Records Office. And there was very little to them apart from the fact that they were photographs. Each had a scrap of paper securely pinned to the upper left hand corner, and on each scrap of paper someone, though in a different hand on each, had drawn a cross. On one of the scraps, beneath the cross, as though to make certainty more certain, a female hand had written: "This is the one."

Clem examined the photographs like a scientist faced with some unknown phenomenon he had to place. Then he looked inquiringly at the sergeant.

"Two people," the sergeant said. "Two people with good memories. They saw a messenger from a bank robbed in Hapton three years ago. And these people's memories were good enough to pick your picture out of six. You, they say, are the man who robbed the messenger from the bank. And now, having seen your picture again, they are quite sure that they'll be able to pick you from a crowd."

The sergeant was definite, clear, deliberate. He left the photographs in Clem's hands, for him to look at.

Clem looked at the pictures, then again he looked at the sergeant.

"After. three years" he said. There was meaning in his tone.

"After three years," the sergeant said. But there was something in the tone in which he too said it.

Clem began to see, and seeing he was outraged.

"They each picked this picture out of six? But what six, Sergeant! Five other people of different age and sex or bald and six feet tall?"

The sergeant returned Clem's gaze. At the same time he shrugged his shoulders in a fashion that indicated something, he did not say what, about the nature of the world.

"Surely you don't think I would stoop to that?"

Clem looked at him in the absolute certainty that he would stoop to it.

"I saw them myself," the sergeant mildly said. "Of course," he said quickly when Clem reacted to that, "this preliminary canter of identity is not the official one. This was only for the evidence for the extradition. The official identity parade will preceed the trial. It's just unfortunate that these people are now convinced that they will be able to identify you when they see you."

It was visible in Clem's face, his thought, his certainty, his knowledge that the sergeant had an irony exceeding all sense of humour. The sergeant could not conceivably be unaware how his identity had been established at his first trial. And now ... He looked around at the pleasant, sunlit square, at the statues of pity and murder and triumph, as though he were facing something monstrous in the possible loss of them. Only it was not that which was monstrous. It was the method, the deliberate repetition, which amounted to a sadistic impulse.

"Sergeant!" the words were torn from him. "If you are doing this—this evidence!" he stared at the pictures. "What possible reason have *you* to think that I had anything to do with the crime at Hapton?"

The sergeant looked at him mildly and did not explain about arithmetic. He left it as something inexplicable, something as unnatural as his sudden appearance in Florence itself had been.

"You don't like prison, do you, Clemens?" the sergeant said irrelevantly. "It's a pity about the climate of opinion back at home. The sentences for robbery with violence are getting bigger all the time, at the same time that the sentence for murder has been reduced to life. A pity, isn't it? The sentence you'll get for this, say nine or eleven years on Dartmoor, will be much the same, though not quite the same, as if you were charged for the other thing."

It was suddenly apparent that Clem was sweating in the sunlight. Perhaps he had decided, at that point, that there was no limit to what the sergeant knew. Yet he was not allowed to guess what the sergeant's intentions were. The sergeant leaned forward, confidentially, across the table, and began to tell him, to repeat as it were, and to continue from where he had ended before he showed the pictures.

"I told you, Clemens," he said intently. "I tried to tell you. I'm a man with a finely chiseled conscience! It's something that's come to me from almost a life-time of other people's stories. People who wouldn't speak to anyone else but who speak to me in strictest confidence. They tell me things that would open your eyes to what is going on. But I can't use what they tell me. I can't quote them, that is to say, or take down what they say in a notebook for use as evidence later. So sometimes, but very rarely, I have to stretch the facts a little, the facts that can be used to substantiate the stories that can't be told, to obtain a conviction— and not always the right conviction—for something that I know to be completely certain. You see how dependent that is on my sense of responsibility and my conscience! And I never do it before I have inter-viewed the man in question. I never do it before I have given him the chance to excuse himself, or deny, or justify his crime. You're lucky in a way! You had to wait a long time, and I had to come a long way to see you!"

"But you don't know!" Clem said, sweating. "You can't possibly know anything that I did!"

The sergeant did not amend his finely over-intimate and gentle and confidential manner.

"I have to interview you first," he said quite mildly. "I wouldn't like to feel I had gained a promotion by a loaded conviction. It's exactly as I told you, because I have a sense of justice. Justice perhaps not in the shape of law, the blind machine, but a better justice, Clem, and one that you above all should recognise: the justice to the man. And I think you know what that means. It means maybe that if you had committed the Hapton crime, and I knew you had committed the Hapton crime, but that was all, I wouldn't act on that. I wouldn't become judge and jury, Clem, for a crime that was cleanly done and in which no mistakes were made! I'm not as hard as the law, you see. I don't feel tempted to bend the straight line for a single error! But *murder*, especially murder afterwards, and *planned* murder, comes into a different category in my own opinion. And it is my opinion! It's my opinion that matters. I hope you see that? Because that is why I want you to talk to me."

Clem looked wildly across the square as though contemplating some sudden flight. "And if I say I have nothing to say" he said.

The sergeant shrugged his shoulders as though Clem had in fact said he had nothing to say. He even moved slightly, pushing back his chair from the table as though prepared to go.

"You know the answer," he said grimly. "You can please yourself. It's up to you. I've offered you the opportunity to explain yourself. You certainly don't need to take it."

He rose from his chair, preceding Clem, not rising after the other, nor following him, but himself showing every indication that the interview was over and that he was about to go away. Before Clem's incredulous gaze he moved round the table, departing, but pausing a moment, and laying his hand for an instant on Clem's shoulder.

"There is a slight difference," he said, "between

the sentence you'd get for the Hapton crime and the one for the other thing. I've been wondering how I can make it up, make justice perfect. I've been wondering for about a year. It isn't difficult I've decided. I won't need to do anything except take my time. It will do itself. You can go, you see. You can go and take up hiding in some slum in Istanbul or Naples. You'll do it, I can see that. *You* won't give yourself up. It's because you hate gaol so much that you'll do your best to stay out of it . . . But that will give you an extension of the sentence just because you'll know it's coming in the end."

The sergeant paused. His words were even more idle now:

"You'll live maybe for months or years in some foreign city, in a slum, with companions lower than the content of the average English gaol . . . But you'll know that Interpol will get you in the end. You'll look round corners, every corner. You'll serve your additional sentence that way. A man with your imagination in those surroundings will feel all the fun they say a fox feels when the hounds are breathing on his heels. Maybe for years. For maybe a lifetime. For a man like you, that will make the difference. You'll realise too late you'd be better in the gaol."

The sergeant looked at Clem with an expression that was wholly indifferent, then turned and began to walk away.

Clem desperately called after him: "Sergeant!"

The sergeant turned and looked back with more scorn than pity but did not come back at first.

Clem waved him to the empty chair.

"I'll talk!" he said. Unexpectedly, his face had taken on a ghastly pallor. "Sergeant, I tell you it wasn't murder!"

"Well, you know yourself," the sergeant said. "You'll do, I suppose, exactly what you must do."

# CHAPTER TWENTY

"SERGEANT!" Clem said. "It wasn't murder. I can see you think it was, but you're making a big mistake!"

The sergeant had returned to the table. He sat down in his chair again, but edgily, as though he were prepared to go away, and his face did not relax its new-found grimness.

"You're telling me it was an accident?" he said. "After all that had gone before, it was an accident at just that time and place? Because if so, you're going to have to say something you haven't said before, before you can convince me."

Clem looked at him for a moment as though he were indeed speculating on the possibility of insisting that it had been an accident. If that was his intention, he saw nothing to reassure him. He looked a moment longer and his eyes seemed to cling to those of the sergeant, not falling but holding to make a vast appeal.

"No, Sergeant. Not that mistake. Another one. A much bigger mistake than that!"

Clem's eyes were indeed haunted, and the sergeant relaxed a little, or if not exactly relaxed, at least looked less as though he were about to get up and go again in a matter of seconds. He would give Clem somewhat longer moments but judge him from moment to moment as he went on.

"You know what I've been telling you, Clemens.

You convince me that it was not murder and I'll think again about that evidence for the Hapton crime. I'll think whether the witnesses were swayed by those photographs and the manner they were presented to them. But you have to convince me, no matter whether it's difficult or impossible. I don't want to be prosecutor, judge and jury, man! But you're too good a liar, Clemens, and you have to pay the penalty of all liars."

"Sergeant!" Clem said, and pressed his clenched fists against the table.

They sat, the sergeant waiting now and prepared to wait: scornful, even a shade contemptuous, but waiting.

"Sergeant," Clem said in a quieter, uncertain voice. "Why do you think I chose this place to live?"

"You had to live somewhere," the sergeant dryly said. "You'd hardly choose England or the Riviera after what happened in both those places."

"There was more than that," Clem said bitterly. "You've asked me to tell you the truth. But do you think I know it?" He hesitated, himself looking up and sideways then, beyond the sergeant and past the sergeant's shoulder. "There's something here, Sergeant. You'll have to turn to look at it. It's something I come to look at every day, to discover what you call the truth."

He went on looking and did not explain, and it was with reluctance that the sergeant turned, also to look, to see in the direction of the loggia, which Clem not he had been facing, across the corner of the sunlit square.

It was not difficult to see what the subject was, for only one of the statues in the loggia stood clear, in the foreground, beneath the shapely arches. There were others in the background. There was the profound pity of the soldier bearing the naked body of the slain. There was the Rape of the Sabine women presented there, priceless yet freely available for inspection, for utility as it were, under the open roof of arches in the public square. There was even the other Rape, the Polyxena, in which the relationship of the bodies was less formal perhaps but infinitely more touching and realistic, the girl tense, with upturned breasts, as she was thrown across the warrior's arm, already aware of what she regarded as her defilement, and the woman, the mother perhaps, imploring and clutching at his knees, while he, caught inexorably in the situation, of necessity must strike at the mother with his upraised sword, or lose, or perish. But all these, from the particular of Clem's chosen table, were only the background to the main work.

It was the bronze Perseus by Cellini which appeared to be in the foreground, in the centre of the archway, the noble work of the noble youth who yet showed humility, who feared the gods. The winged helmet and winged feet of a classical figure were allied to a touching youth, a finely worked object showing, on the artist's part, a Christian love for the actual in a slender naked body that antiquity could never claim. And yet this youth, born from Athens perhaps by way of Donatello, was in that situation which antiquity had regarded as most dire for mortal man. A decapitated female body was at his feet, from which the lifeblood gushed, and his sword in the right hand was still held forward, not withdrawn yet from the act. And in his left hand, high above him, he held the Medusa's gory head.

Clem looked and the sergeant looked, and from their expressions alone it was possible to see that in the same object they saw different things. Clem stared at something he already knew too well. The sergeant frowned, turned back, and asked him:

"Well?"

Clem went on looking.

"Why me, Sergeant?" he said. "Can't you see I had no option?"

That at least was honest, and the sergeant looked, and did not answer.

Clem made a desperate attempt at statement:

"Don't you see, Sergeant, that she was a Medusa, that her very glance froze men and turned them to stone? Yet she was a living woman underneath! She didn't know the effect of her genteel manner, of the clothes she wore, of the very thoughts that someone had taught her were so right and proper—all she knew was that she who was so perfectly what she had been taught to be had only to approach a man and he turned to stone!"

Clem was insistent, desperate, and for the sergeant it was an actual shock. He had expected an appeal for pity, but what he was asked for was pity for the victim, and the speaker was the one he regarded as the accused.

And yet, in an instant, he saw the parallel. Perhaps it was the smell of flowers, of sunlight-faded blooms which, faint though it was, Clem had found oppressive in the sunlit Italian square. But the sergeant was not in Italy for an instant. He was back at home and watching Emma Smith, a woman walking as she came to him down a street, a woman born in a northern, misty climate, but not a faded flower amid the grey roofs and street lamps and nonconformist chapels, but a woman of flesh and blood and feeling, whose very appearance, before she came to him, and the sound of whose voice when she did come, would freeze him, alienate with something like fear, with the necessity to escape, the very sympathy he might feel for her. For an instant there was something frightening in the reality of the vision, in the fact that he was not thinking of the general term, the "victim", or even, since that was what Clem made her, the "accused", but an actual woman who had walked and thought and felt, and whose existence, too obviously, could not be abolished or eradicated merely by her death.

"If you could only understand!" Clem said, "Her anguish, her helplessness, her refusal to believe! Because she was right! She really was that epitome of rectitude and propriety that her teachers had held up to her as a model. And yet men did not love her! They fled from her. They feared her and escaped her as they might some unnatural object! So what could she do? What could she do, except believe that the evidence of her sense was not true? Men did not hate her. You must see that she had to believe that! Men loved her secretly and wished to rape her. It was the only door she could go through, the one that led to the unreal world, the one she populated from her imagination only. You ask me for the truth, yet how can I convey to you the pity of such a woman?"

Temporarily at least, the sergeant was lost. The truth, if it was the truth, was so different from anything he had imagined that he could hardly grasp the solid facts, the events that he knew he knew. He looked at the man across the table and for a moment he found him hard to see and understand.

"And yet you killed her?" he said. "You say that, that you killed her?" For whatever else he was saying, Clem, by saying it was not murder, had said exactly that.

"Yes, I killed her," Clem said. He gave the sergeant a smile that was wan and ageless and experienced as the buildings around them in the square. "Why not say it? I'll tell you though it will do no good. You won't believe me. You can't believe me. It's something beyond your experience, so you can't know it."

"But why?" the sergeant said. "What are you telling me? That you loved her or you hated her?" He looked at Clem helplessly, remembering all he had told Clem about the decision that he had to make. "Or is it," he said with an attempt at insight, "that you only understood her, that you knew exactly what you killed?"

Clem regarded the sergeant with a curious, helpless smile, a comment on one who had adopted a moral tone.

"Both," he said, bitterly. "I hated her and loved her. Do you think I could do anything else but hate her at my trial? I only thought I understood her then, as I watched her as the trial went on. I knew the facts, the facts of her, but not the experience that lay behind her! Have you ever thought of what the people feel who advocate the cat and physical punishment for crimes of violence? I felt that then. I wanted to wake her up! To make her feel, however slightly, some actuality—to give her some knowledge of what she was doing, that other people existed beside herself—that other people existed, actually, outside her mind! But

I was egotistic too. I was in those days! I wanted her to understand that I was at least as respectable and full of rectitude as she was. I, who had spent my whole life working! It was the mistake about me I could not bear, and naturally I hated her! I swore I would never forget her, that I would make her feel some day!"

The sergeant's intelligence of what had happened seemed to swim in a sea of feeling. He saw not the Italian square, the two of them leaning forward and talking earnestly across a table, but a stark young man in a crowded court room, a woman who testified with eyes inturned, who did not see.

"So you did!" he said. "Clemens, I'm trying to understand. You know that. I can't promise anything. I'm trying to understand. But you found her afterwards." His mind had leaped ahead. "It wasn't accident. You sought her out. You went back to her when you came out of gaol?"

"Did I ever come out of gaol?" Clem said. "I've tried to tell you, but will you ever understand what prison meant to me?"

The sergeant stared, said nothing.

"Prison," Clem said distinctly, "was for me a torture of the damned. But you've got the nature of the torture wrong, you prison officers and warders and do-gooders. You imagine that solitary confinement would be the worst you could inflict on a man like me! You do worse than that. In solitary—and I was in solitary once—you can even think. But in prison life, two or three in a cell and warders at the door, you can't even do that! The waste of time, of life, is total and intolerable. It is humiliating. Everything about prison is humiliating. That is the essence of the punishment you give. The prisoner can neither do nor think nor have any wishes of his own. Your system was designed not to cure, but to break a man! But suppose you don't break him? And I can tell you in truth you almost always don't! How then can the prisoner recover his self respect? How can he recover from the humiliation he has suffered? Would you believe that before I went to prison I had never once thought of committing any crime? Yet when I came out it was with that one idea. It wasn't Emma Smith I hated then! The hatred was vaster and more generalised. I knew then. I hated all of you!"

"I was right about one thing," the sergeant said quietly across the table. "You were the one who did the Hapton crime."

Clem looked at him scornfully and bitterly. "How right you are, Sergeant, to stick to the simple facts. You never lose sight of the ball for a single instant. But what are you trying to do? To prove something, to pin something on me, or to understand? Because you'll never achieve any understanding that way."

The sergeant nodded. He was prepared to go on, to go on to something that was bigger than the robbery at Hapton.

Clem went on because he must. It was not a story he would have told willingly at any time.

"I met Emma Smith again," he said. "It was not quite by chance. We were in the same part of the country. Our paths were bound to cross. When they did, I looked her up in the telephone directory and found out what I could of her. I hated everyone, remember. I thought I hated her the most. I met her again. You know the arrangements I made so that I could meet her without too much danger to myself. All I needed was to be aware of the danger that I ran.

I had not been aware the first time. I took good care the second. And when I knew what she was, I thought I would destroy her."

"You mean you decided to murder her?" the sergeant said.

Clem looked at him. His expression was scorn and pity.

"Murder a woman who was suffering as she was?" he said. "That would have been love, not hatred. I decided to destroy her morally, in the place where it would hurt: her respectability."

The sergeant's lips twisted.

"You wonder how and why I can tell you that?" Clem said. "I'll tell you. Because it didn't work. It didn't work at all as I thought it would! She was not at all what I thought her, and nor was I!"

"It led to Monaco," the sergeant said, quietly now, not scornfully, but insisting on the conclusion.

"It led to Monaco by a long way round!" Clem said. "And this is the part of the story you won't believe. You won't believe because you won't understand or try to understand! You won't realise how inevitable it was that when Emma and I came together, I with my hatred for you all, and she who was so helpless and vulnerable in her mad imagination, it was two against the world. How could I hate her? She wasn't *there* enough to hate. Mentally she was about as solid as a drifting cloud. *It wasn't her fault.* She should have been cared for, not asked to testify at a trial. And she had nothing to do with the rest of you. It was you, the police and the public who were to blame. She and I were bound together by an accident, the accident of your blindness. If I hated you, I had to love her. If I loved her, I had to hate you. Because

193

what I discovered was simply this: *that if you knew what she was you would persecute her even more deliberately and thoughtlessly and cruelly than you persecuted me.* Simply, you would put her in a mad house."

The sergeant was facing difficulties, and Clem could see he was.

"So you married her," the sergeant said, "because you loved her?"

"I married her," Clem said, "because I needed to protect her! To protect her from you. Because you were circling round her like a moth round a flame and at any moment were going to discover exactly what she was. And besides, there was triumph in it. You can put it that way. That I married her to spite you. I don't claim—and you must understand this—I don't claim I knew exactly what I was doing. I hadn't been trained in psychiatry! You may think I'd seen a lot of life by then, but in fact I hadn't. I'd lived very narrowly. I thought she would get better when I married her! I thought that she'd be a shade more normal, and that we'd be able to go on living—well, somewhere. We had the money. We'd be a monument. A kind of triumph over you. There was something pathetic, I now see, in my need for that."

The sergeant looked at Clem closely. "I've noticed that," he said. "You are telling this in the past tense. You don't feel these things now? You're trying to tell me that you've changed?"

"Not quite," Clem said, quietly now. "Not I who changed. I was changed. When I discovered the truth. I discovered it on our honeymoon. There's no need to go into details. I've read about it. Afterwards. I'd released something, and the details were obscene.

She was going mad all right. The only way I could keep her from you was to murder her. I found myself in cold blood thinking of an act of murder. I thought of it quite coldly, what a woman like her would suffer —she never in all her life had anything but her respectability to value—if she were certified as insane. She was not the type who would know it as an illness or realise there was no moral stigma attached to that. I thought of it, and I realised I could not do it. Then I would look at her and feel a rush of pity and know I had to. I was very deliberate in the end. I felt humility too. I knew the part I had played, my own mistake, in encouraging her. I realised, at the time of the . . . of the death, that I was as fallible as you were. I didn't hate her any more. I could hardly love what she was becoming. I didn't hate you any more. I was drained out. I came here and saw this." He pointed at the statue. "It held me. It was the clearest expression I had ever seen of what it was necessary to do with a Medusa. If you look at the boy, you'll see there's nothing outrageous about him. He's in action, but he's not exactly wild with triumph. He's doing what is necessary, and that is all. He doesn't know yet what it will be like afterwards, but I could tell him. He'll be a law-abiding citizen. He'll do nothing else."

The sergeant had turned sideways in his chair and was brooding on the statue amid the steady scent of flowers.

# CHAPTER TWENTY-ONE

THE sergeant stirred. He turned and looked across the table, across the undisturbed table-cloth and the coffee which, after all, neither he nor Clem had drunk.

"Clem," he said quietly, "I don't know how to put this."

Clem did not stir for a moment. He went on staring across the corner of the square. Then he turned and looked directly at the sergeant.

"You mean you don't believe it?" he said. "I told you I hardly thought you would. You mean you're going to have me arrested for the Hapton crime? To pay for what I've already told you that I paid for?"

"No," the sergeant said. "I believe it all right. I believe that that is the way you saw it. But the way you saw it isn't everything. There's a slight discrepancy with the facts."

Clem nodded. He was prepared for some slight discrepancy with the facts. He could not tell everything in a single effort.

"I'm going to tell you the truth, Clemens," the sergeant said. "And it's going to be hard to bear."

Clem looked at him steadily, not denying anything since there was nothing to deny, but not accepting anything. He had shot his bolt. He had told the truth as he saw it, and he was prepared to hold to it.

"Just one little thing to begin with," the sergeant

said. "You say you live here quietly. That you won't 'do anything'—and I suppose that means crime—again. But isn't that a little easy? Since you can live, however modestly, on the interest on fifteen thousand pounds that you got from your wife and the other crime?"

Clem did not flinch.

"I'm not sure I know what you mean," he said. "It's true I have money. But it's money that's come to me more by accident than any other way. After all, I would have had money by now if I had been able to follow the career I started. It was only an accident, the accident of going to gaol, that took that from me. If you could put me back in that life, I'd be glad to give up the money I have now."

The sergeant nodded.

"You have a point," he said. "Not a good one, but a point. I knew another man once who lost his living by an accident. He was married with three children and everything in his home was on hire purchase. He was doing fine until he got cancer, but that is by the way. It's only that according to you that man would have had the right to commit any crime, the more so as the only beneficiaries would be his wife and children."

"What are you getting at, Sergeant?" Clem said.

The sergeant made a gesture that indicated the irrelevance of what he said:

"In Asia," he told Clem, "two million people die every year from the associated diseases of malnutrition. A child could often be saved if the father could steal a shilling. Are you sure, Clem that you are awake yet, that you know the world you're living in?"

Clem frowned at him in the Italian sunlight. "Is this

metaphysics, Sergeant? Because if it is I don't quite follow you."

The sergeant paused and lengthily considered him.

"I still don't think you have it," he softly said at last. "That life is better if we play it by the rules. It's bad that way. We know it is. But if we don't obey them it gets far worse."

Clem answered his gaze. "No," he said, "I don't see that. I think you were nearer to it when you spoke of justice to the man. To the man who has lost, or to the starving child."

The sergeant idly nodded. "Yes," he said. "Justice to the man. I'd agree to that. Except that no man has the right to judge his own case. If the rules are to be broken, it must be someone else who must break them for him."

Clem considered it.

"You mean you will break them for me!" he said.

The sergeant tried to make his answer neither too hasty nor too slow. Needless suspense was not his policy. He answered:

"No."

It lay there solidly, the thumbs-down signal.

Clem had nothing to say. He tried desperately not to show even that he had not been expecting it.

"Look at your first crime," the sergeant said quite gently. "The one of which you claim you were innocent. You heard a woman screaming in the night. You did not go to her. Have you ever thought how little importance was attached to the testimony of Emma Smith? She alone would not have sent you to a long gaol sentence. It was the plain facts that were against you: the evidence that everyone had heard the scream except you. You who were near it and had good hearing. You were given ample opportunity to say you heard it. But you didn't because you couldn't. You couldn't say you heard it without explaining you were too much of an egotist to go to answer it. You thought you could get off without that."

Clem looked puzzled at that point: not shocked exactly but distinctly puzzled.

"After your first crime, of which you were innocent but guilty," the sergeant said, "came the second of which you were guilty but innocent."

Clem stared, with something like horror.

"Oh, don't think I don't believe you, Clemens!" the sergeant said. "I believe that your primary object in that crime was not to get money! You've confessed almost with pride that your object was spite—spite just as it was when you formed the idea of marrying Emma Smith. But what kind of a man are you? One who regards spite, when it is your own spite, as the mean and despicable emotion that it is? You're not. I've listened to you and I haven't heard a trace of that horror you should have felt to discover that you—you who have an admiration for yourself!—should have had that feeling!"

The sergeant was leaning forward now, still careful, not allowing his voice to rise, but visibly intent, pinning Clem and disrobing him inexorably, point by point.

Clem, on the other hand, was showing more violent signs of strain. His face was haggard. He was showing strain now that he had not shown in the moment the sergeant had told him that he would not excuse him. It was not the fact that he apparently resented, but the steady stripping, the deliberate exposition of the why.

"Sergeant! I told you that I—"

But the sergeant had turned, moving steadily in his chair and indicating the statue that lay half round behind him.

"How convincing your story of your third crime might have been, Clemens, if that statue had not been there, if you hadn't lived here and come each day to see it, to convince yourself of a story that even you can't quite believe!"

"Sergeant!" Clem had pushed back his chair. He showed every evidence of getting up, of going away, of refusing to listen any longer to an exposition which to him at least might have seemed to be verging on the sacrilegious, and that regardless of the consequences.

The sergeant leaned across the table and gripped the wrist of the hand with which he pushed against the table edge.

"Is that what you're going to do" Clem said. "Condemn me and convict me on evidence you know is faked because I mentioned a statue, a work of art, as a means to explain to you something you couldn't understand!"

His tone was outrage. It was a scene that was developing in the sunlight of the quiet square.

"Yes!" said the sergeant, and there was nothing gentle about him now. "I condemn you because you almost took even me in, with a work of art!"

Clem struggled, then suddenly realised he could gain nothing by commotion. It was visible in him, the knowledge that the sergeant was taunting him, was provoking a scene in which either or both of them might be arrested, and held by the Italian police perhaps, until the papers came.

"Your third crime," the sergeant said intently, still reaching across the table, when he saw Clem's sudden quietness. "The one of which you were guilty and known to be guilty and for which you will be punished." His grip tightened with the intentness of his voice. "Poor Emma Smith. With you, because of your first trial, as the only one in the world who knew her as she was. You, released from gaol with knowledge like that! Had she known, she might well have died and saved us both a host of trouble. Because you had no need to get her in your power, Clemens. She was in your power. And you had your way with her . . ."

The sergeant's eyes sought those of the other man and were met by naked fright. Clemens' were looking at him as though he was a madman.

"You had your way with her, didn't you, Clemens? You married her . . . You had your way with her in other words, in the most public way . . . For spite . . . With Emma Smith. A mad woman whom it had never crossed your heart you might forgive. And then you murdered her . . . Publicly. Sacrificially. Before a crowd of people. Why had it to be before a crowd of people? Do you know that? In public, so they saw? And yet so you would remain untouched? The complete revenge? But not complete. There was one other item. Her respectability was not the only thing that Emma loved. She also loved her money: and it was that that made it essential that you should marry her before you did it. So that her money, the only thing she valued, should be delivered to you, also publicly, for all the world to see or hear about, by the Probate Court. That was really complete! You had done it all! And it wasn't for pity, Clemens. It was vicious and malicious. It was desperate and despicable and abject and obscene. It was murder and it was calculated murder, a murder that had been calculated to the Nth degree. You can go now, Clemens! You can go: I've finished with you!"

The sergeant did not so much release Clem as shake him off, and it was he who went, standing for a moment, looking down at him, wordlessly at the wretched man. Then he went, walking steadily out of the café, leaving Clemens to the square, the sunlight, the table, the statue, and the pervasive scent of flowers.

# CHAPTER TWENTY-TWO

"NOW, Herbert," Mrs. Huntley said, "you positively must explain."

It was the sergeant and his wife now who were sitting at the table in the café in the Piazza. They were both sitting on the same side of the table and looking at the Perseus statue, and the sergeant, comfortable, with a glass of Marsala wine before him, which Mrs. Huntley always called his depraved taste, seemed little inclined to explain anything to anyone.

"I don't suppose he's here?" Mrs. Huntley said, looking round quickly all about them. "I don't suppose there's any chance he'll overhear us!"

"Oh, no," the sergeant said. "He's left the city. Heading south, I believe. At a guess I'd say his destination is North Africa. Maybe Algiers."

He sat on comfortably, but as for explanation, it was not forthcoming.

"Herbert," Mrs. Huntley firmly said.

"What do you want to know?" the sergeant said. He showed a distinct and positive interest in the Perseus statue. Besides, he knew how hard she would find it to frame the questions.

"I want to know," Mrs. Huntley said decisively, "Exactly why, when you came to me the other day, you wanted me to forge two crosses on different scraps of paper and write beneath one of them 'This is the one'. And don't tell me it's regular police business. It's something nefarious that you've been up to."

Her husband tried the spicy wine. To him it seemed singularly harmonious with the sunlit Italian scene.

"I told you," he said. "He's a murderer. He's the only successful murderer I know. I wanted to put the fear of God in him."

"And do you think that that will be enough?" Mrs. Huntley was outraged.

"Oh, yes," said the sergeant. "I think it will. He really believes it, you see. He thinks the police are after him. And since there is no possible way he can find they are not short of asking them and offering to give himself up, he's going to go on believing it all his life."

"But surely—I mean, after years of hiding, won't he get tired of it—won't he do just that?"

"He might," the sergeant said. He looked judicially at the Perseus as though the secret of Clem's future actions were contained in the physical aspect of the figure or features of that noble yet humble youth. "But I don't think he will. He's allergic to prison, you see. He isn't quite the type. For some inexplicable reason he thinks that prison is some peculiar kind of hell that's designed for him. But so is hiding."

Mrs. Huntley took straight vermouth when they were abroad. She regarded it almost as a fortunate stroke of fate, and a release from temptation, that they could not afford it when they were at home. She drank half a glass full to assist her thinking process.

"Poor man," she said. "To spend his life in hiding. I hardly think it's enough for a murderer all the same."

"He's a very sensitive murderer," the sergeant said. "He can't even murder unless he first convinces himself that it is for the best possible motives. And even afterwards—I told you about this statue."

"But guilty? You're sure of that?"

"Oh, most definitely guilty."

"In that case," said Mrs. Huntley, having felt the effect of the vermouth, "it's a confession of weakness on your part that you can't arrest him, charge him and convict him."

"I suppose it is," the sergeant said amicably. He had finished his Marsala. Having caught the eye of the waiter in the distance he held up fingers, indicating two more drinks.

"But don't you feel conscience-stricken about it?" Mrs. Huntley said. After twenty years of marriage she was still interested in her husband.

The sergeant watched the waiter and breathed with satisfaction when he saw him appearing with the drinks. "Drink up," he said to his wife, and watched her drain the other half glass before the waiter reached them. With another full glass before him he felt more expansive and easy in his mind.

He looked around the square. The buildings, it was true, were ancient. And the Michelangelo David was a copy, a facsimile of the original that was kept in the Accademia where it was protected from the decoration of the birds and the erosion of the weather. But the statues under the loggia were originals and there was something more friendly than outrageous about the Neptune fountain. Even the café had got fresh flowers.

"No," he said. "I don't feel conscience-stricken about my inability to trap a murderer. I think I have trapped him. Besides, I'm not always sure it is the murderer who is most guilty."

"Just to think," Mrs. Huntley said, "that I work half the year so we can afford foreign travel when it has this effect on you."

"How can there be justice," the sergeant said, "when there is no court to decide those cases where the victim is the guilty party?"

"He'll be a saint in a minute," she said with a glass in her hand. "I'm surprised you even discomposed him."

The sergeant considered the Perseus statue.

"I more than discomposed him," he said softly. "I broke down the story he'd been telling himself about it. Perhaps that's the most fatal punishment you can give to any man. Those stories usually survive a court. That's the way the guilty becomes the injured party."

"That's too much," said Mrs. Huntley firmly. "I give it up. Now where are you taking me for lunch today?"

"The café across the Ponte Vecchio?"

"No, we'll have dinner there. We're going to do the Pitti Palace this afternoon."

"Then why not here?" the sergeant said. "I rather like," he confessed, "the feeling of remaining in possession of the field of battle."

"Herbert!" said Mrs. Huntley. She sighed. "Oh, well," she said. "You can ask the waiter for the menu."

# THE PERENNIAL LIBRARY MYSTERY SERIES

### Delano Ames

**CORPSE DIPLOMATIQUE**       P 637, $2.84
"Sprightly and intelligent."
           —*New York Herald Tribune Book Review*

**FOR OLD CRIME'S SAKE**       P 629, $2.84

**MURDER, MAESTRO, PLEASE**       P 630, $2.84
"If there is a more engaging couple in modern fiction than Jane and
Dagobert Brown, we have not met them."       —*Scotsman*

**SHE SHALL HAVE MURDER**       P 638, $2.84
"Combines the merit of both the English and American schools in the
new mystery. It's as breezy as the best of the American ones, and has
the sophistication and wit of any top-notch Britisher."
           —*New York Herald Tribune Book Review*

### E. C. Bentley

**TRENT'S LAST CASE**       P 440, $2.50
"One of the three best detective stories ever written."
           —Agatha Christie

**TRENT'S OWN CASE**       P 516, $2.25
"I won't waste time saying that the plot is sound and the detection
satisfying. Trent has not altered a scrap and reappears with all his old
humor and charm."       —Dorothy L. Sayers

### Gavin Black

**A DRAGON FOR CHRISTMAS**       P 473, $1.95
"Potent excitement!"       —*New York Herald Tribune*

**THE EYES AROUND ME**       P 485, $1.95
"I stayed up until all hours last night reading *The Eyes Around Me,*
which is something I do not do very often, but I was so intrigued by the
ingeniousness of Mr. Black's plotting and the witty way in which he spins
his mystery. I can only say that I enjoyed the book enormously."
           —F. van Wyck Mason

**YOU WANT TO DIE, JOHNNY?**       P 472, $1.95
"Gavin Black doesn't just develop a pressure plot in suspense, he adds
uninfected wit, character, charm, and sharp knowledge of the Far East
to make rereading as keen as the first race-through."       —*Book Week*

## Nicholas Blake

**THE CORPSE IN THE SNOWMAN**                     P 427, $1.95
"If there is a distinction between the novel and the detective story (which we do not admit), then this book deserves a high place in both categories."
                                        —*The New York Times*

**THE DREADFUL HOLLOW**                     P 493, $1.95
"Pace unhurried, characters excellent, reasoning solid."
                                        —*San Francisco Chronicle*

**END OF CHAPTER**                     P 397, $1.95
". . . admirably solid . . . an adroit formal detective puzzle backed up by firm characterization and a knowing picture of London publishing."
                                        —*The New York Times*

**HEAD OF A TRAVELER**                     P 398, $2.25
"Another grade A detective story of the right old jigsaw persuasion."
                                        —*New York Herald Tribune Book Review*

**MINUTE FOR MURDER**                     P 419, $1.95
"An outstanding mystery novel. Mr. Blake's writing is a delight in itself."
                                        —*The New York Times*

**THE MORNING AFTER DEATH**                     P 520, $1.95
"One of Blake's best."
                                        —Rex Warner

**A PENKNIFE IN MY HEART**                     P 521, $2.25
"Style brilliant . . . and suspenseful."          —*San Francisco Chronicle*

**THE PRIVATE WOUND**                     P 531, $2.25
[Blake's] best novel in a dozen years . . . . An intensely penetrating study of sexual passion. . . . A powerful story of murder and its aftermath."
                                        —Anthony Boucher, *The New York Times*

**A QUESTION OF PROOF**                     P 494, $1.95
"The characters in this story are unusually well drawn, and the suspense is well sustained."
                                        —*The New York Times*

**THE SAD VARIETY**                     P 495, $2.25
"It is a stunner. I read it instead of eating, instead of sleeping."
                                        —Dorothy Salisbury Davis

**THERE'S TROUBLE BREWING**                     P 569, $3.37
"Nigel Strangeways is a puzzling mixture of simplicity and penetration, but all the more real for that."          —*The Times Literary Supplement*

**THOU SHELL OF DEATH** P 428, $1.95
"It has all the virtues of culture, intelligence and sensibility that the most exacting connoisseur could ask of detective fiction."
—*The Times* [London] *Literary Supplement*

**THE WIDOW'S CRUISE** P 399, $2.25
"A stirring suspense. . . . The thrilling tale leaves nothing to be desired."
—*Springfield Republican*

**THE WORM OF DEATH** P 400, $2.25
"It [The Worm of Death] is one of Blake's very best—and his best is better than almost anyone's." —Louis Untermeyer

### John & Emery Bonett

**A BANNER FOR PEGASUS** P 554, $2.40
"A gem! Beautifully plotted and set. . . . Not only is the murder adroit and deserved, and the detection competent, but the love story is charming." —Jacques Barzun and Wendell Hertig Taylor

**DEAD LION** P 563, $2.40
"A clever plot, authentic background and interesting characters highly recommended this one." —*New Republic*

### Christianna Brand

**GREEN FOR DANGER** P 551, $2.50
"You have to reach for the greatest of Great Names (Christie, Carr, Queen . . .) to find Brand's rivals in the devious subtleties of the trade."
—Anthony Boucher

**TOUR DE FORCE** P 572, $2.40
"Complete with traps for the over-ingenious, a double-reverse surprise ending and a key clue planted so fairly and obviously that you completely overlook it. If that's your idea of perfect entertainment, then seize at once upon *Tour de Force*." —Anthony Boucher, *The New York Times*

### James Byrom

**OR BE HE DEAD** P 585, $2.84
"A very original tale . . . Well written and steadily entertaining."
—Jacques Barzun & Wendell Hertig Taylor, *A Catalogue of Crime*

### Henry Calvin

**IT'S DIFFERENT ABROAD**                    P 640, $2.84

"What is remarkable and delightful, Mr. Calvin imparts a flavor of satire to what he renovates and compels us to take straight."

—Jacques Barzun

### Marjorie Carleton

**VANISHED**                    P 559, $2.40

"Exceptional . . . a minor triumph."

—Jacques Barzun and Wendell Hertig Taylor, *A Catalogue of Crime*

### George Harmon Coxe

**MURDER WITH PICTURES**                    P 527, $2.25

"[Coxe] has hit the bull's-eye with his first shot."

—*The New York Times*

### Edmund Crispin

**BURIED FOR PLEASURE**                    P 506, $2.50

"Absolute and unalloyed delight."

—Anthony Boucher, *The New York Times*

### Lionel Davidson

**THE MENORAH MEN**                    P 592, $2.84

"Of his fellow thriller writers, only John Le Carré shows the same instinct for the viscera."                    —*Chicago Tribune*

**NIGHT OF WENCESLAS**                    P 595, $2.84

"A most ingenious thriller, so enriched with style, wit, and a sense of serious comedy that it all but transcends its kind."

—*The New Yorker*

**THE ROSE OF TIBET**                    P 593, $2.84

"I hadn't realized how much I missed the genuine Adventure story . . . until I read *The Rose of Tibet*."                    —Graham Greene

### D. M. Devine

**MY BROTHER'S KILLER**                    P 558, $2.40

"A most enjoyable crime story which I enjoyed reading down to the last moment."                    —Agatha Christie

### Kenneth Fearing

**THE BIG CLOCK** P 500, $1.95

"It will be some time before chill-hungry clients meet again so rare a compound of irony, satire, and icy-fingered narrative. *The Big Clock* is . . . a psychothriller you won't put down." —*Weekly Book Review*

### Andrew Garve

**THE ASHES OF LODA** P 430, $1.50

"Garve . . . embellishes a fine fast adventure story with a more credible picture of the U.S.S.R. than is offered in most thrillers."
—*The New York Times Book Review*

**THE CUCKOO LINE AFFAIR** P 451, $1.95

". . . an agreeable and ingenious piece of work." —*The New Yorker*

**A HERO FOR LEANDA** P 429, $1.50

"One can trust Mr. Garve to put a fresh twist to any situation, and the ending is really a lovely surprise." —*The Manchester Guardian*

**MURDER THROUGH THE LOOKING GLASS** P 449, $1.95

". . . refreshingly out-of-the-way and enjoyable . . . highly recommended to all comers." —*Saturday Review*

**NO TEARS FOR HILDA** P 441, $1.95

"It starts fine and finishes finer. I got behind on breathing watching Max get not only his man but his woman, too." —Rex Stout

**THE RIDDLE OF SAMSON** P 450, $1.95

"The story is an excellent one, the people are quite likable, and the writing is superior." —*Springfield Republican*

### Michael Gilbert

**BLOOD AND JUDGMENT** P 446, $1.95

"Gilbert readers need scarcely be told that the characters all come alive at first sight, and that his surpassing talent for narration enhances any plot. . . . Don't miss." —*San Francisco Chronicle*

**THE BODY OF A GIRL** P 459, $1.95

"Does what a good mystery should do: open up into all kinds of ramifications, with untold menace behind the action. At the end, there is a bang-up climax, and it is a pleasure to see how skilfully Gilbert wraps everything up." —*The New York Times Book Review*

### Michael Gilbert (cont'd)

**THE DANGER WITHIN** P 448, $1.95
"Michael Gilbert has nicely combined some elements of the straight detective story with plenty of action, suspense, and adventure, to produce a superior thriller." —*Saturday Review*

**FEAR TO TREAD** P 458, $1.95
"Merits serious consideration as a work of art."
—*The New York Times*

### Joe Gores

**HAMMETT** P 631, $2.84
"Joe Gores at his very best. Terse, powerful writing—with the master, Dashiell Hammett, as the protagonist in a novel I think he would have been proud to call his own." —Robert Ludlum

### C. W. Grafton

**BEYOND A REASONABLE DOUBT** P 519, $1.95
"A very ingenious tale of murder . . . a brilliant and gripping narrative."
—Jacques Barzun and Wendell Hertig Taylor

**THE RAT BEGAN TO GNAW THE ROPE** P 639, $2.84
"Fast, humorous story with flashes of brilliance."
—*The New Yorker*

### Edward Grierson

**THE SECOND MAN** P 528, $2.25
"One of the best trial-testimony books to have come along in quite a while." —*The New Yorker*

### Bruce Hamilton

**TOO MUCH OF WATER** P 635, $2.84
"A superb sea mystery. . . . The prose is excellent."
—Jacques Barzun and Wendell Hertig Taylor, *A Catalogue of Crime*

### Cyril Hare

**DEATH IS NO SPORTSMAN** P 555, $2.40
"You will be thrilled because it succeeds in placing an ingenious story in a new and refreshing setting. . . . The identity of the murderer is really a surprise." —*Daily Mirror*

**DEATH WALKS THE WOODS** P 556, $2.40

"Here is a fine formal detective story, with a technically brilliant solution demanding the attention of all connoisseurs of construction."
—Anthony Boucher, *The New York Times Book Review*

**AN ENGLISH MURDER** P 455, $2.50

"By a long shot, the best crime story I have read for a long time. Everything is traditional, but originality does not suffer. The setting is perfect. Full marks to Mr. Hare." —*Irish Press*

**SUICIDE EXCEPTED** P 636, $2.84

"Adroit in its manipulation . . . and distinguished by a plot-twister which I'll wager Christie wishes she'd thought of."
—*The New York Times*

**TENANT FOR DEATH** P 570, $2.84

"The way in which an air of probability is combined both with clear, terse narrative and with a good deal of subtle suburban atmosphere, proves the extreme skill of the writer." —*The Spectator*

**TRAGEDY AT LAW** P 522, $2.25

"An extremely urbane and well-written detective story."
—*The New York Times*

**UNTIMELY DEATH** P 514, $2.25

"The English detective story at its quiet best, meticulously underplayed, rich in perceivings of the droll human animal and ready at the last with a neat surprise which has been there all the while had we but wits to see it." —*New York Herald Tribune Book Review*

**THE WIND BLOWS DEATH** P 589, $2.84

"A plot compounded of musical knowledge, a Dickens allusion, and a subtle point in law is related with delightfully unobtrusive wit, warmth, and style." —*The New York Times*

**WITH A BARE BODKIN** P 523, $2.25

"One of the best detective stories published for a long time."
—*The Spectator*

### Robert Harling

**THE ENORMOUS SHADOW** P 545, $2.50

"In some ways the best spy story of the modern period. . . . The writing is terse and vivid . . . the ending full of action . . . altogether first-rate."
—Jacques Barzun and Wendell Hertig Taylor, *A Catalogue of Crime*

### Matthew Head

**THE CABINDA AFFAIR** P 541, $2.25
"An absorbing whodunit and a distinguished novel of atmosphere."
—Anthony Boucher, *The New York Times*

**THE CONGO VENUS** P 597, $2.84
"Terrific. The dialogue is just plain wonderful."
—*The Boston Globe*

**MURDER AT THE FLEA CLUB** . P 542, $2.50
"The true delight is in Head's style, its limpid ease combined with humor and an awesome precision of phrase." —*San Francisco Chronicle*

### M. V. Heberden

**ENGAGED TO MURDER** P 533, $2.25
"Smooth plotting." —*The New York Times*

### James Hilton

**WAS IT MURDER?** P 501, $1.95
"The story is well planned and well written."
—*The New York Times*

### P. M. Hubbard

**HIGH TIDE** P 571, $2.40
"A smooth elaboration of mounting horror and danger."
—*Library Journal*

### Elspeth Huxley

**THE AFRICAN POISON MURDERS** P 540, $2.25
"Obscure venom, manical mutilations, deadly bush fire, thrilling climax compose major opus.... Top-flight."
—*Saturday Review of Literature*

**MURDER ON SAFARI** P 587, $2.84
"Right now we'd call Mrs. Huxley a dangerous rival to Agatha Christie." —*Books*

### Francis Iles

**BEFORE THE FACT**                                    P 517, $2.50

"Not many 'serious' novelists have produced character studies to compare with Iles's internally terrifying portrait of the murderer in *Before the Fact,* his masterpiece and a work truly deserving the appellation of unique and beyond price."                         —Howard Haycraft

**MALICE AFORETHOUGHT**                               P 532, $1.95

"It is a long time since I have read anything so good as *Malice Aforethought,* with its cynical humour, acute criminology, plausible detail and rapid movement. It makes you hug yourself with pleasure."

—H. C. Harwood, *Saturday Review*

### Michael Innes

**THE CASE OF THE JOURNEYING BOY**          P 632, $3.12

"I could see no faults in it. There is no one to compare with him."

—*Illustrated London News*

**DEATH BY WATER**                                    P 574, $2.40

"The amount of ironic social criticism and deft characterization of scenes and people would serve another author for six books."

—Jacques Barzun and Wendell Hertig Taylor

**HARE SITTING UP**                                   P 590, $2.84

"There is hardly anyone (in mysteries or mainstream) more exquisitely literate, allusive and Jamesian—and hardly anyone with a firmer sense of melodramatic plot or a more vigorous gift of storytelling."

—Anthony Boucher, *The New York Times*

**THE LONG FAREWELL**                                 P 575, $2.40

"A model of the deft, classic detective story, told in the most wittily diverting prose."                          —*The New York Times*

**THE MAN FROM THE SEA**                              P 591, $2.84

"The pace is brisk, the adventures exciting and excitingly told, and above all he keeps to the very end the interesting ambiguity of the man from the sea."                                        —*New Statesman*

**THE SECRET VANGUARD**                               P 584, $2.84

"Innes . . . has mastered the art of swift, exciting and well-organized narrative."                               —*The New York Times*

**THE WEIGHT OF THE EVIDENCE**                        P 633, $2.84

"First-class puzzle, deftly solved. University background interesting and amusing."                          —*Saturday Review of Literature*

### Mary Kelly

**THE SPOILT KILL**            P 565, $2.40
"Mary Kelly is a new Dorothy Sayers. . . . [An] exciting new novel."
                      —*Evening News*

### Lange Lewis

**THE BIRTHDAY MURDER**         P 518, $1.95
"Almost perfect in its playlike purity and delightful prose."
            —Jacques Barzun and Wendell Hertig Taylor

### Allan MacKinnon

**HOUSE OF DARKNESS**          P 582, $2.84
"His best . . . a perfect compendium."
    —Jacques Barzun & Wendell Hertig Taylor, *A Catalogue of Crime*

### Arthur Maling

**LUCKY DEVIL**                  P 482, $1.95
"The plot unravels at a fast clip, the writing is breezy and Maling's
approach is as fresh as today's stockmarket quotes."
                —*Louisville Courier Journal*

**RIPOFF**                      P 483, $1.95
"A swiftly paced story of today's big business is larded with intrigue as
a Ralph Nader-type investigates an insurance scandal and is soon on the
run from a hired gun and his brother. . . . Engrossing and credible."
                       —*Booklist*

**SCHROEDER'S GAME**           P 484, $1.95
"As the title indicates, this Schroeder is up to something, and the un-
ravelling of his game is a diverting and sufficiently blood-soaked entertainment."                     —*The New Yorker*

### Austin Ripley

**MINUTE MYSTERIES**           P 387, $2.50
More than one hundred of the world's shortest detective stories. Only
one possible solution to each case!

### Thomas Sterling

**THE EVIL OF THE DAY**         P 529, $2.50
"Prose as witty and subtle as it is sharp and clear. . .characters unconven-
tionally conceived and richly bodied forth . . . . In short, a novel to be
treasured."            —Anthony Boucher, *The New York Times*

### Julian Symons

**THE BELTING INHERITANCE**  P 468, $1.95
"A superb whodunit in the best tradition of the detective story."
—August Derleth, *Madison Capital Times*

**BLAND BEGINNING**  P 469, $1.95
"Mr. Symons displays a deft storytelling skill, a quiet and literate wit, a nice feeling for character, and detectival ingenuity of a high order."
—Anthony Boucher, *The New York Times*

**BOGUE'S FORTUNE**  P 481, $1.95
"There's a touch of the old sardonic humour, and more than a touch of style."  —*The Spectator*

**THE BROKEN PENNY**  P 480, $1.95
"The most exciting, astonishing and believable spy story to appear in years.  —Anthony Boucher, *The New York Times Book Review*

**THE COLOR OF MURDER**  P 461, $1.95
"A singularly unostentatious and memorably brilliant detective story."
—*New York Herald Tribune Book Review*

### Dorothy Stockbridge Tillet
### (John Stephen Strange)

**THE MAN WHO KILLED FORTESCUE**  P 536, $2.25
"Better than average."  —*Saturday Review of Literature*

### Simon Troy

**THE ROAD TO RHUINE**  P 583, $2.84
"Unusual and agreeably told."  —*San Francisco Chronicle*

**SWIFT TO ITS CLOSE**  P 546, $2.40
"A nicely literate British mystery . . . the atmosphere and the plot are exceptionally well wrought, the dialogue excellent."  —*Best Sellers*

### Henry Wade

**THE DUKE OF YORK'S STEPS**  P 588, $2.84
"A classic of the golden age."
—Jacques Barzun & Wendell Hertig Taylor, *A Catalogue of Crime*

**A DYING FALL**  P 543, $2.50
"One of those expert British suspense jobs . . . it crackles with undercurrents of blackmail, violent passion and murder. Topnotch in its class."
—*Time*

### Henry Wade (cont'd)

**THE HANGING CAPTAIN**  P 548, $2.50

"This is a detective story for connoisseurs, for those who value clear thinking and good writing above mere ingenuity and easy thrills."

—*Times Literary Supplement*

### Hillary Waugh

**LAST SEEN WEARING . . .**  P 552, $2.40

"A brilliant tour de force."  —Julian Symons

**THE MISSING MAN**  P 553, $2.40

"The quiet detailed police work of Chief Fred C. Fellows, Stockford, Conn., is at its best in *The Missing Man* . . . one of the Chief's toughest cases and one of the best handled."

—Anthony Boucher, *The New York Times Book Review*

### Henry Kitchell Webster

**WHO IS THE NEXT?**  P 539, $2.25

"A double murder, private-plane piloting, a neat impersonation, and a delicate courtship are adroitly combined by a writer who knows how to use the language."  —Jacques Barzun and Wendell Hertig Taylor

### Anna Mary Wells

**MURDERER'S CHOICE**  P 534, $2.50

"Good writing, ample action, and excellent character work."

—*Saturday Review of Literature*

**A TALENT FOR MURDER**  P 535, $2.25

"The discovery of the villain is a decided shock."  —*Books*

### Edward Young

**THE FIFTH PASSENGER**  P 544, $2.25

"Clever and adroit . . . excellent thriller . . ."  —*Library Journal*

# If you enjoyed this book you'll want to know about
# THE PERENNIAL LIBRARY MYSTERY SERIES
Buy them at your local bookstore or use this coupon for ordering:

| Qty | P number | Price |
|---|---|---|
| | | |
| | | |
| | | |
| | | |
| | | |
| | | |
| | | |
| | | |
| | | |
| | | |
| | | |
| | | |
| | | |
| | | |

|  | postage and handling charge | $1.00 |
|---|---|---|
| | _____ book(s) @ $0.25 | _____ |
| | **TOTAL** |  |

**Prices contained in this coupon are Harper & Row invoice prices only.** They are subject to change without notice, and in no way reflect the prices at which these books may be sold by other suppliers.

**HARPER & ROW, Mail Order Dept. #PMS, 10 East 53rd St., New York, N.Y. 10022.**
Please send me the books I have checked above. I am enclosing $_____ which includes a postage and handling charge of $1.00 for the first book and 25¢ for each additional book. Send check or money order. No cash or C.O.D.s please

Name_____

Address_____

City_____State_____Zip_____
Please allow 4 weeks for delivery. USA only. This offer expires 1/31/85. Please add applicable sales tax.